FREEDOM
Beyond the Sea

FREEDOM
Beyond the Sea

WALDTRAUT LEWIN

Translated from the German by
Elizabeth D. Crawford

DELACORTE PRESS

Published by
Delacorte Press
an imprint of
Random House Children's Books
a division of Random House, Inc.
1540 Broadway
New York, New York 10036

Visit us on the Web! www.randomhouse.com/teens
Educators and librarians, for a variety of teaching tools, visit us at
www.randomhouse.com/teachers

Library of Congress Cataloging-in-Publication Data
Lewin, Waldtraut
    Freedom beyond the sea / Waldtraut Lewin ; translated from the German by
Elizabeth D. Crawford.
        p. cm.
    Summary: To escape the Inquisition, Esther Marchadi, the sixteen-year-old
daughter of a murdered Jewish rabbi, disguises herself as a boy and joins the crew
of Christopher Columbus's "Santa Maria."
    ISBN 0-385-32705-6
    1. Columbus, Christopher—Juvenile fiction. [1. Columbus, Christopher—
Fiction. 2. Jews—Spain—History—Ferdinand and Isabella, 1479–1516—Fiction.
3. Seafaring life—Fiction.] I. Crawford, Elizabeth D. II. Title.
PZ7.L584195 Fr 2001
[Fic]—dc21
                                                        2001017279

The text of this book is set in 12.25-point Legacy Serif Book.

Book design by Alyssa Morris

Manufactured in the United States of America

October 2001

10 9 8 7 6 5 4 3 2 1

BVG

FREEDOM
Beyond the Sea

This is the day of sorrow and despair. This is the ninth day of Av, the day on which the temple of Jerusalem was destroyed for the second time and the Jewish people had to leave their homeland. Since then they wander among the peoples of the world.

Reckoned according to the Jewish calendar, it is the year 5252. Today, on the ninth day of Av—as reckoned by the Christian calendar, August 2, 1492—Jews must once again flee their homeland.

At midnight of this day, by edict of Their Catholic Majesties Ferdinand and Isabella, rulers of the Kingdom of Castile, there must be not one Jew left in Spain.

The Moors have been conquered in the south of the country, and now it is the Jews' turn. According to the will of the Inquisition, tomorrow Spain will be inhabited only by pure-blooded, faithful Christians. Only those who accept baptism can remain.

Many have had themselves baptized. The others have fled. Portugal swiftly closed its borders. Now everyone is rushing to the southern harbors. The price of a crossing to France or Italy, to Morocco or Tunis quickly doubled, then rose higher and higher.

All the ships are overloaded. As to whether those passengers will ever arrive—who knows? The captains look more like pirates than sailors, and their miserable tubs could suffer a shipwreck at any moment. Those who escape drowning could be sold into slavery. Who among the Jews of Castile will make it through safe and sound?

All are filled with fear, and so am I.

But the three ships lying here at anchor in Palos, in the bay of the Río Tinto, are in fine shape. There are two caravels and a *nao,* a large vessel, the *capitana,* the flagship of the group. Still, the men going aboard here this evening seem no less depressed and desperate than the Jewish families in Cadiz, Valencia, and Barcelona. They don't know if they will ever reach their destination.

But I'm going with them. And for me, the day of despair is at the same time the day of hope.

IT IS NOW ONE HOUR BEFORE MIDNIGHT. We aren't sailing till morning, of course, but the admiral of the little fleet has given the order for the entire crew to be on board by midnight. The captain of one of the caravels,

Martín Pinzón, protested. It's not the custom on a Christian voyage to board the night before. The men want to take leave of their wives and families or spend a last night in the tavern. But the admiral is standing by his order.

The boys beside me say he suffered one of his famous attacks of rage, during which his pale face flushes and he curses in his mother tongue, Italian, badly enough to bend the beams.

Captain Pinzón usually turns on his heel and leaves at outbursts like that. But he obeys. There's no love lost between the admiral and Pinzón, says one boy. The other replies, yes, but they need each other.

They grin and wonder what could be the reason for ordering all the men to be on board tonight.

"Maybe so they can't run away at the last minute," says the first boy, with a conspiratorial wink.

They seem terribly sharp.

But I can imagine why the admiral wants to have his ship manned tonight. I've looked around at the prospective crew. Among these "pure-blooded, faithful Christians," there might be many a one like me, who fears the adventure of an unknown destination less than the Spain of our fathers.

WE SIT ON THE WALL ALONG THE QUAY, dangling our legs. The night is soft, and the stones of the pier give back the sun's warmth from the August day just past.

There are four of us grummets, the ship's boys of this fleet. But there are only three ships.

We have lots of time to wait. The embarkation of the men goes strictly by order of rank. The captains, the shipowners, and the pilots each get their people aboard; sometimes someone is exchanged; it takes time. We're at the very bottom. The last. The boys for the dirty work. I'm one of them, a moses.

"Moses!" says one of the boys, and he spits. "They name us like one of them damned Jews."

I keep my face indifferent. I've learned to do it in these terrible last six months, to show no reaction when they abuse the Jews.

Two of the boys are from here, from Palos. They know the Pinzón family, which has supplied two captains for this journey. They're not going to sea for the first time; they're veterans. Their hands are large and callused, with broken fingernails, and their naked feet are dirty and tough. I still wear sandals all the time because I'm not used to going barefoot, and though my hands certainly have gotten some scratches recently, for a ship's boy who handles ropes, they're much too soft and delicate.

The two boys are named Juan and Pedro, and when they ask me my name, I also say Pedro. Every other boy here is named Pedro. I'm on the ship's list as Pedro Fernández from Zaragoza.

"Zaragoza," says big Juan. He's surely about sixteen. "So then you're a landlubber?"

"I was just born there," I answer. "My father was a seaman, and I've sailed with him ever since I can remember."

The truth is, I saw the sea for the first time a week ago, when I got myself signed on. To do it, I had to bribe the fleet secretary, Rodrigo de Escobedo, with all the money I had left and hand over the letter of introduction I carried with me. And even then everything was still uncertain. It still is uncertain. We are four ship's boys for three ships.

The third boy comes from Moguer, the place the Niños come from, the owners of the third ship. That boy is named Alonso. He's fourteen years old, thin and tall, and I took an instant dislike to him because he carries around in his pants pocket, wrapped in a leather cloth, a long object he claims is the little finger of a Jew that he fished out of the ashes at the site of a burning. He claims a finger like that brings luck and protects against sickness even more than the amulet with the picture of the Blessed Virgin that he wears around his neck.

I just don't believe that about the finger because I can't believe it, and the others also make scornful gestures behind his back. But what clearly is true is that he's sailed with Juan Niño to Cape Verde. When we first met, he peeled back his shirt with pride and displayed the scars left on his back by the provost's cat-o'-nine tails. That means they don't dillydally on the Niños' ship. But it's not much different on the other ships, either.

We sit there and wait. Juan collects small pebbles from the edge of the pier and throws them at the dogs that are wandering about. When he hits one, it hunches up or turns around howling, without understanding where the attack is coming from, and Juan breaks into laughter. He thinks it's funny. The other two are quiet. All three are afraid about this trip, but no one shows it.

Alonso breaks the silence. "You know the *capitana* ship's doctor is one of them baptized Jew swine, a Marrano? I know him. He's from Moguer, too, like me. Six months ago the hook-nosed brute was still running around in a long caftan with a beard. The beard's gone now, but you can tell by the nose. And by the stink."

No one answers him. Everyone is much too busy with waiting and with his own thoughts to take up this otherwise popular theme. I breathe again. As for stink, I think the three of them could hardly be surpassed. Never washing, and on top of that, garlic from supper.

Juan keeps on throwing his stones, and Pedro digs in his nose with a finger. Clearly he finds the next awkward problem there. "So," he says. "There are three ships. And there are four of us grummets. How's that supposed to work?"

Alonso shrugs. "I don't care what you do," he says indifferently. "In any case, I'm sailing with the *Niña*. Juan Niño is my master and Yáñez Pinzón is my captain."

"I'm going with the second Pinzón, on the other

caravel," Juan declares. "That's how it is! And besides, the Quinteros are there. My father always sailed under the Quinteros until he died. They're the owners and hire the bosun. They'll take me."

"The other caravel"—that's the *Pinta*, Martín Pinzón's ship. Right at the very beginning I made a fool of myself in front of the others by speaking of three caravels. Now, of course, I know that the third is a *nao*, a tubby ship, more cumbersome than the other two. People say she gets mulish under sail. She used to be named *La Gallega*, but the admiral renamed her.

"So that leaves us two Pedros for the flagship," I say, trying to kick my legs as carelessly as the others.

Silence. Then says the other Pedro, "Don't know why the *capitana* needs two ship's boys. Is one of us supposed to wipe the crazy Genoese's behind for him?"

We measure each other with stares. This Pedro is bullish and square-built, with small eyes under straight brows. The mood is not good. I try to defuse it by laughing. "Wait," I say. "It'll straighten itself out somehow."

"I don't care," says my namesake. "It doesn't matter to me what you do. I'm from here, from Palos, and Martín Pinzón signed me on, and I'm sailing with him." He looks quickly at Juan, but Juan doesn't say anything. "I'll tell you this," Pedro goes on. "I listened carefully to what Señor Pinzón said. Where we're going is the land of gold. They even roof their houses with gold tiles there because they're so dumb they think it's worthless. We'll all make our fortunes. We'll come back rich. Then no more working your tail off." He's breathing hard.

"True," says tall Alonso with the whip scars. "*If* we come back."

And then there's silence again, even thicker than before. My heart is beating so hard from agitation that it hurts. If only there isn't an argument, a fistfight! But luckily they have other things on their minds. Juan cranes his neck and says, "Time to go a little closer. Being eager always makes a good impression. So let's get going, in the name of the Virgin and all the saints."

The three hop off the wall, crossing themselves quickly with the carelessness of long practice, and I try to do the same.

WE PUSH OUR WAY through all the people standing around on the quay. The harbor is full of people. Women are hanging on their husbands' necks and weeping. They carry their sleeping children in shawls on their backs. The men are standing in line, assuming gruff faces so as not to show how uneasy they feel.

I move through these scenes without being moved by them. I've seen other farewells in the last half year and other griefs. No one here is being forced to go to sea. They all want to get gold, the gold of the Indies.

Together with the three boys I station myself at the end of the line. I'm feeling sick with excitement.

Now I can see the admiral. He's sitting at a table between four large bull's-eye lanterns made of horn. With him are the fleet secretary, Rodrigo de Escobedo, who entered me on the rolls, and one of the royal officials. The admiral's white hair billows out from under his beret and glows in the light. They say he already had white hair by the time he was thirty.

The list is lying in front of him on the table. For a ship's register, this is a very precise list. After all, the sailors hiring on are in the service of the Crown. So every maravedi paid out will be carefully entered in the book.

Nevertheless, there has never been anything farther from the truth than this list. I suspect I'm not the only example. But I'm a glaring one.

In this register it states that I am called Pedro Fernández, from Zaragoza, and that I was born into an orthodox Christian family. But I am Jewish and have not ever, like the other examples on the list, been baptized for show. I also come not from Zaragoza but from Córdoba. And I am not called Pedro Fernández but Esther Marchadi. This is the lie that tops all the others: I'm hiring on as a ship's boy, and I'm a girl.

AS LONG AS NO ONE GETS THE IDEA I should undress, I can easily conceal this. I'm much too thin for my sixteen years, and I have boy's hips and so little bosom that it can be hidden without any trouble under a big shirt.

9

What I've been through in recent months has made me even more gaunt. My long face, with its thick eyebrows and large nose, has grown hollow-cheeked. I look like any other of the half-starved street boys in Palos or Moguer. They also have short, curly black hair like mine, brown skin, and dark eyes. This is how pure-blooded Castilians look.

As a girl, I'm a homely thing. As a boy, I might just get away with it. Anyhow, my body won't betray me. My hands and feet, yes, they are treacherous. My gestures. My speech. So I talk very little and keep to myself.

THE PINZÓN BROTHERS, the captains, are standing at the end of the gangplanks that lead to their ships, meeting their crew one by one, as it were, as they muster them in. Now we're close enough to see everything very clearly. The Pinzóns are standing to the left and right of the admiral. Martín is the elder and the head of the seafaring family. He has a crooked, arrogantly wry mouth, which snakes through his dark stubble of beard like a scar, and eyebrows that grow together. He looks hard and overbearing. I've heard that you can get whip scars like Alonso's under the command of the younger, friendlier, curly-haired Yáñez Pinzón, too, so strictly speaking, I don't know if he's any better.

Beside the admiral, acting as his spokesman, is the owner of the *capitana,* Juan de la Cosa, a gray-haired man from the Basque country with a broad nose and the neck of a steer. He likewise wears a stern look. I've already heard that he's in a fury at the admiral, who supposedly told him that his ship is really too tubby for exploring trips and he took it only because there wasn't any other available.

My comrades are busy running him down, but in whispers. "Whoever heard of a foreigner directing a *capitana*! Basque immigrants, baptized Jews, Portuguese, Venetians—a bunch of rascals! Even the admiral himself is a Genoese! And he wants to give orders to us pure-blooded Andalusians! Lucky we're going on *our* ships!"

That's Alonso again, the great foreigner-hater, and Juan chimes in. "Things usually go along pretty well on the *Pinta* and the *Niña*. Andalusian sailors of the old stamp, my uncle says. The Pinzóns, the Niños, the Quinteros."

Pedro nods morosely and looks enviously at the two of them. He'll probably have to go on the "dirty foreigner's" ship. With me . . .

"You know," he says through clenched teeth, "they should take all of them, right now where they're standing, and pull down their trousers and make sure they really aren't circumcised goddamned Jew swine, Marranos and Conversos!"

I let out a gasp of fear. I have to cough and curse in a

voice that's really breathless but which I try to make as rough as these boys'. *"Hombre!* That'd be something! That many bare asses would outshine the moon!"

They laugh at my joke. I'm hot all over. I feel sick.

And then we're there. The last ones. In front of me is the pale face of the admiral and his glowing silver hair.

Now it's quiet everywhere. The men on the ships are standing at the railing and looking out over the quay, and the relatives—the women and children, the brothers and fathers—are also entirely silent. The children are hanging on to their mothers' apron strings or asleep in their arms and shawls. The women have pulled their veils up to their eyes.

From the Church of San Jorge the clock strikes eleven.

"Now just the grummets, Your Grace," says the secretary. He also talks softly. "Juan Molino to Don Martín. Alonso Esposito has already sailed with Don Yáñez. That leaves two Pedros for your ship."

"Two Pedros, how inconvenient," says the admiral. He speaks Spanish with a slight accent. "We'll exchange one. Anyhow, why does the ship need two? Space is tight enough as it is."

"That is true," says Rodrigo de Escobedo, in whose pocket my maravedis have landed, and without looking at me, he takes the feather from behind his ear to dip it into the ink. "We'll cross off one Pedro. But which one?"

The admiral, who until now has been toying with his

gloves, raises his eyes and looks at us. His eyes, which are gray, gray like clouds, gray like the ocean he means to sail over, eyes such as I have never seen in anyone before, travel between me and the other Pedro, back and forth. I have a strange feeling. I take a deep breath and hear myself make a whistling sound. And then, to my horror, I discover that I've taken a step forward and am saying something directly to those gray eyes that seem to rivet me. I say, "The Lord be praised. I can read and write, also in Latin."

The gray eyes are turned on me, unblinking, and I do not close mine.

"I can do that, too," says Rodrigo, the fleet secretary. "You won't be needed for that, boy." And the others laugh, but not the admiral. Then he says, "Perhaps he could be of use to me as my personal servant or page, Don Rodrigo. We'll take them both. But we'll exchange the other Pedro so we have no confusion. He may go on the *Niña*. We'll take this other one. This Alonso."

I bow deeply and think to kiss the admiral's hand, but he's already turned and left. He's the only one spending the night on land, in prayer, they say, in the cloister of La Rábida.

Together with Alonso I run up the gangplank to the ship. I can hear him snorting with rage and disappointment behind me. It won't be easy to be in such a small space with him. He's sure to make me pay for his not being with his beloved Yáñez Pinzón. But I'm not worried about that. Not now, anyway.

I'm safe. One hour before the murderous expulsion edict against the Jews goes into effect, I've left the soil of Spain and am on board a ship. I, a Jewish girl, am on board the *Santa María,* the flagship of Admiral Christopher Columbus.

Chapter Two

I'm walking on the deck of a ship for the first time. If the others knew that, all these seamen with their sun-darkened faces, golden earrings, red wool caps, and their sacks of belongings on their shoulders . . . Even if they've only ever worked on the coastal ships until now and always sailed within sight of land, each of them knows the difference between a jib and a gaff and a topgallant and a mizzen and is familiar with everything that has to be done on board. I have no idea at all. I've only imagined from books and pictures and tried to learn it, the way a person can learn to swim on land. I only hope I don't make any blunders that are too huge. I don't want to get whipped or keelhauled.

Now I've cleared the first hurdle. I've gotten where I am with some courage and a great deal of luck. Perhaps as the page of the admiral I can avoid the work of the seamen. . . .

I stand here, and it seems to me that a whole mountain has fallen from my heart. Yet still I know that after getting through the big difficulty, a hundred small ones will follow. Something new, every day, every moment.

Suddenly all around me these men have become wildly busy, and I can make no sense of it. They run back and forth, calling out jokes or crudities to each other, cursing in various dialects, jostling and pushing me here and there.

"Hey!" I hear. "Don't stand around, boy!" That was Andalusian. "Move the hawser out of the way!" cries someone else with a Basque accent. Hawser? What hawser? "Are you planning to take root there, snotnose?"

Slowly I catch on to what they are doing. They're finding places for themselves to sleep, and with their respective countrymen, of course. An Andalusian is driven with curses from a corner that the Basque faction has taken for itself. A group of four sinister-looking fellows who say nothing at all spread themselves out amidships. They have long boarding cutlasses in their belts.

Everyone is apparently against everyone else. Fifteen men have found sleeping places—the rest, I learn, are the first watch and are under the orders of a red-haired man with broad shoulders named Chachu, who speaks Basque, just like the owner. Evidently he's the mate. He assigns duties, giving them first to the Andalusians.

Alonso isn't spared and has to go aloft to the lookout, from which he sends dirty looks at me.

A group of gentlemen push their way through to the aftercastle—not that the sailors show any sort of deference to those fine folks. On the contrary, I have the feeling that some intentionally ram them in the side with their elbows. Among them is the fleet secretary, so well known to me, Escobedo, who no longer "knows" me—luckily.

I send a fervent prayer to the god of my forefathers. I have to get along with all these men. I must know precisely what their activities and tasks are. That is my only chance not to attract attention. Not attracting attention is everything. Then maybe I can keep out of their way, fit myself in.

In the meantime, I now notice, all the sleeping places are gone. At least the good ones. This little ship—even if it's bigger than all the others—has no cabins for sailors. That would be wasteful. People just spread out wherever they can find a place. And those who are strong can spread out more. Everyone else has to put up with it. Of course, you can stretch out on the cargo below deck, but the air down there is thick enough to cut with a knife. So long as it's warm and doesn't rain, the men would rather stay above deck. Only, what a lot of stuff there is lying around here! Ropes, tackle and blocks, rolled-up replacement sails, hawsers, water pumps, barrels whose contents I don't know, the anchor, and the anchor winch. Everything is crowded together around the ship's hatch in the middle, and I see why. It's the only flat surface. The deck slopes like a donkey's back. Anyone lying at the edge always runs the danger of rolling down, with only the ship's edge to keep him from a plunge into the water. And that's exactly what's in store for me. Because every other place is taken.

I stow my small bundle behind the shrouds. It will serve me as a pillow. I have nothing else. I'll brace my feet against a coil of rope so as not to slide off.

Most men have mats in their seabags and a cloak to cover them. It's still warm. Even much too warm. I try to stretch out as well as I can, cross my arms under my head, and gaze at the starry heavens.

The men around me are talking. Hardly any of them can get to sleep in this overly hot night before the beginning of the great voyage. They talk of the land of gold that they anticipate and call the Indies. Their seabags will be stuffed full with red gold when they return. It's why they're risking the voyage.

I want to go to the Indies, too. But I'm not looking for gold there. And it appears to me that a few others on board this ship are also looking for something other than gold. Perhaps the man from Genoa is one of them, too, Christopher Columbus, whom here in Spain they call Cristóbal Colón. The admiral of the ocean seas with the eyes of cloud and sea.

I know that now I must fall asleep quickly, fall asleep

in a way that prevents the memory pictures from appearing and following me into my dreams. Such pictures don't let one sleep or wake. They must not come out. I must put them away entirely. They are hidden in my bundle on which I am lying, the bundle that is firmly tied. They lie on the bottom of the sea and will never come to the surface again. They are buried deep, deep down in a vineyard, and a large stone is rolled over the place.

This way is right, Esther, I tell myself. You're living, you're breathing. The Lord has saved you. Praised be the name of our God. *Boruch atto elohenu.*

Then I count until sleep comes. When I'm counting, I don't have to think of anything else. Yes, I fall asleep.

I START UP. That's a bell! The condemned criminals' bell they sound as the Inquisition's victims climb to the stake, that dreadful, chilling, monotonous tolling. And I smell the smoke! They are going to burn, oh, they are all going to burn!

At the very last moment I suppress the scream trying to work its way out of my throat by pressing both hands against my mouth. You must not betray yourself, Esther! Never, do you hear? my father says.

Then I see the streaks of dawn in the sky and the pale stars over me. The smoke I smell is drifting to me from the open firebox on the stern, the stove. And the bell is not the condemned criminals' bell that signals the burning of a heretic but the ship's bell for the changing of the watch. I am aboard the *Santa María*.

A shrill male voice squawks, "Blessed be the soul immortal—preserved by God in every peril—blessed be the day that breaks—and God th' Almighty Who all things makes."

Everyone around me falls on his knees to say the Paternoster and the Ave Maria, and I hasten to do the same. Don't stand out, whatever you do!

All my limbs ache. Of course I rolled toward the edge of the deck in my sleep, arms and legs swaying over the water. The coil of rope against which I'd braced my feet is gone. Clearly someone wanted it for a pillow. They tossed my bundle on top of me.

I've barely said amen and crossed myself when someone is poking me roughly in the ribs with a foot.

"Get up, lazybones. It's your watch," says my mate, Alonso. His face is pale with weariness under its freckles. "I turned the sandglass once more, though that really should have been your job. Just make sure you don't forget it! Go on, make space."

Without asking, he sits down on my bundle. He's holding a piece of hard cheese with a sardine on it, obviously breakfast. He chews noisily.

Service on a ship is divided into three time periods, that much I know. So I have to turn the sandglass sixteen times, and then it's another shift's turn to sail the ship. I hope I don't miscount! It would get me a beating, and not a slight one, either, if the watch just finishing had to work longer than necessary.

Meanwhile the squawking voice chants, "God grant us good days, good voyage, good speed to the ship, to my lord captain, and good shipmates. Let us make a good voyage, you gentlemen of the aftership and also you gentlemen of the foreship." Evidently I'll be hearing the same thing every morning.

Naturally, there are others on board who, like us grummets, are very low down in the ship's hierarchy. They are the peons, men who are not allowed to become full sailors and who have to do the dirty work—and how much of that there is, I can't even imagine at this point. They're the ones who've never learned to tie an expert knot or to reef a sail, men who just carry out orders. One of them has obviously gotten far enough to be able to recite this morning speech. The peons are the ones I most fear. Everyone tramples on them, so they will be on the lookout for someone whose hair they can pull, backside they can kick, or ears they can box. And those will be the ship's boys, obviously.

Luckily, no one is paying any attention to me, and I'm being very careful not to make myself noticeable in any way. I'm not hungry, either, so I don't have to report to the storeskeeper to get *vizcocho* with garlic or cheese and sardines. Not yet, anyway. But I'm tormented by thirst. The water barrels are below deck in the stores room, the *bodega*. The real sailors all have some kind of battered pot in their seabags to be able to carry water or soup. I don't, of course. So in an unobserved moment I put my mouth under the spigot of the water barrel and drink in long drafts. The water is still fresh and cool, it's still drinkable.

Something is happening up on deck. I hear commands and the fast tapping of many naked feet. I hurry to the hatchway and climb up through the hot, stuffy air to the deck.

I stick my head out of the hatch just in time to catch the great moment. The whistle of the Basque mate shrills in my ear, and in front of me I see the naked, gnarled calves of the men, their blackened, battered, horny feet. Each is standing at his post. As quick as a ghost, I slip sideways behind a great coil of rope.

Juan de la Cosa, the owner, hat off, is receiving the commander, while the mate trumpets, *"Almirante a bordo!"*—admiral on board.

Columbus has an instinct for grand entrances. He is wearing a bright red velvet cape and, in the manner of the Genoese, has a gold chain draped carelessly several times around his neck. In his hand he holds the Christian symbol, the rosary, its beads constantly gliding through his gloved fingers as he prays. His white hair billows out from under a beret adorned with medals. I am clearly not the only member of his ship's company regarding him with a kind of thrill. There's something about him you can't describe, and these seamen, who aren't exactly noted for their finer feelings, sense it, just as I do.

Columbus proceeds to the poop, the raised afterdeck of the flagship, and says, without raising his voice: "In the name of God, set sail."

Yes, he speaks softly. But his voice is heard clearly everywhere, and obviously it's also understood on the two caravels in front of us at the pier.

The ship's owners give their orders. The men insert the capstan in the capstan crab and begin to haul up the anchor. The pulleys screech in the blocks like seagulls as the gigantic white linen masses of the sails rise and the banner of the expedition is run up the mast: a white silk cloth, on which stands a green cross and the initials of Their Majesties under golden crowns. Amid the sailors' rhythmic chanting, which accompanies all their tasks, the ships move languidly away from the wall of the quay.

But the sails hang slack, and the banner doesn't unfurl. The wind is still. Wearily the ships drift down the Río Tinto with the current and pass the sand banks of Saltes.

"Give way, there, boy," someone says to me. Again orders are bawled. They free the great long oar to maneuver through the estuary.

"Not a good sign, a departure like this," growls a voice near me. "Day for the gulls."

He doesn't look unfriendly, a sinewy young fellow with a thick head of hair—one of the Basques, from his accent.

I gather my courage. "What's that, *señor*?" I ask. "What does 'day for the gulls' mean?"

He inspects me sideways while he does something or other with the ropes that I don't understand—it looks very expert. "You a landlubber?" he asks, but the question doesn't have the hostile undertone it did with the ship's boys, and he doesn't wait for my reply to explain. "When the sky is without wind and the sea is without waves, the gulls can get busy: They build their nests out on the water, from clusters of algae. Nothing disturbs them. No wind, you understand. And it's a Friday, too. If only this goes well!" He frowns and again turns to the braces.

I twist my head to look back at the admiral. He's standing on the poop, unmoving. The sultriness of this oppressive day, noticeable even so early in the morning, appears to be caught in his red cloak, which looks as if it were on fire. He gives no orders. I hear the captains of the caravels as they carefully maneuver their vessels through the narrow bottleneck between pine-dotted sand dunes. The *pilato mayor* of our ship, the navigator Pero Niño, is clearly following the movements of the caravels, which are in the lead. There are no orders being given on our *Santa María* at the moment. Juan de la Cosa is silent, perhaps because he expects the admiral to give the orders. And the admiral? He stands there, looking ahead.

And then the land falls away, and in front of us, as far as the eye can see, stretches a smooth, leaden gray surface. Before us lie the ocean seas, clasped in the embrace of the burning heat of the early August day.

Yes, it is dull and depressing. All the men are quiet. Most are certainly afraid. And what is going on in the admiral's head, only he knows. But I have entered into a new freedom, a new life.

Spain, the country that doesn't want me, has spit me out. It has annihilated more of my people than would have been killed in a war. But I am outside. It came very close to me yet once more, threateningly close. No wind. And a canal so narrow, as if it wanted not to let us go but to draw us back into its deadly embrace. But I have escaped.

I can begin anew.

WHAT A DAY, and what a night! During the last twenty-four hours I've wished probably a hundred times I'd stayed on land—or that I'd die. I didn't know a person could feel so miserable.

The shallow strip of coast is still in sight, but the day for the gulls is already over. A soft breeze has come up, and the crew is rejoicing. I hear how the ship comes alive. The sails and the masts hum and groan, the wood of the planking creaks. The *Santa María* is singing her song.

It seems to me that a wild confusion reigns on board. Evidently no one knows exactly what's what; thousands of details have to be settled; the men jostle, get in each other's way, and curse; commands are bellowed. I have my job. I have to keep an eye on the sandglass. Besides, the Basque I spoke with before is in charge at the firebox. He seems to be something like the ship's cook and prepares the only warm meal there is here each day. There are chickpeas with mutton bones today, and I know I'm lucky. Today I can eat, too. When it comes to the salt pork they're carrying in a barrel in stores, I'll have to think up an excuse, for I'm not allowed to eat pork, according to our dietary laws. But I don't have to give any thought to that today. The Basque has put me to work chopping up firewood for him and stirring the soup pot—an easy job, which I do happily. I'm even looking forward to eating, until—yes, until I catch sight of the two other ships.

The breeze has freshened. Off to our side I see the *Pinta* and the *Niña,* two pitch-black nutshells dancing on the swells, their sails billowing over them as if they wanted to fly right away. And then I feel the first uneasiness in my stomach. We're dancing in just the same way. Until now I've been amused by the movements of the giant seesaw on which we find ourselves, smilingly balancing my movements, catching myself at the right moment when we go down, bracing my legs to ride the motion to the top. Everything has gone well. But all at once my mouth is terribly dry, and I have to swallow convulsively; something seems to be twisting in my stomach.

26

The Basque—his name is García—glances sideways at me. "Well, boy, has it started?" I nod. He grins good-naturedly. "Nobody escapes having it when he sails for the first time. And even the old hands have it now and then. *Mal de mer*, seasickness. They say it has two phases: In the first stage you're afraid you'll die. In the second you wish you were dead after all."

I smile in disbelief. I can still smile. García purses his lips. "Look there," he says, pointing to the leeward. "If it isn't our fine gentlemen passengers!"

Our fine gentlemen passengers! Two men in very respectable garb, their dark clothes in sharp contrast to the bright linen shirts of the crew, are hanging over the railing, vomiting their hearts out.

"Who are they?" I ask weakly as I battle my rebellious stomach.

"The royal provost the admiral's dragging along—word has it he's cousin to the admiral's mistress—and a Don Gutiérrez from the court. No one knows what his real business here is. Oh, and now there's the interpreter, too!"

García knows everything. But I can't listen properly anymore. With both hands pressed over my mouth, I also stumble to the railing.

The rest of the day is only a blur. It's unbearable, and the worst is when I watch the others eat. My stomach feels as if it's suspended inside me by a string. I bring up only green bile and am shaken by convulsions of vomiting and blinding headaches. I squat, a heap of misery, in the shadow of the topgallant and rock back and forth. The others jeer, but their jeers are restrained. They all know well what it feels like, and now and then I see a sailor, too, one hand pressed to his mouth, the other to his belly, sneak over to the side of the ship. Apparently nobody is feeling really good. Far away, through my misery, I hear them giving advice—each one has a different remedy for the sickness, each swears by his own. They vary from drinking brine to saying the Paternoster backward. One says you should press your thumb very firmly between the middle and ring fingers, count to twenty, and then let go. I try it and imagine that the illness actually does lessen a bit. But then it comes over me again, so bad that I almost faint.

Through it all I manage to take care of the sandglass at the right time, even though I am afraid I might keel over each time. Diego, the *despensero,* the storeskeeper, his beard already gray, feels sorry for me and takes over calling the glass for me. He's the one, too, who urges me to eat something. "That way, you at least have something to throw up," he says calmly. "And besides, you'll feel better. Even if you don't believe it."

So I choke down a piece of *vizcocho,* the unleavened bread preserved in salt, and then greedily reach for the *bojito,* the clay jug he hands to me, lift it over my face, and let the stream of water run into my mouth from a distance. Luckily I've learned to do that during the last six months. It tastes wonderful, and then I realize that the storeskeeper has mixed the water with the strong yellow wine that we also have on board. I'm grateful to him, for I really do feel a little bit better—until the next time I have to run for the railing.

My watch is over at noon, and now I don't have to worry about the sandglass any longer. Relieved, I crouch in my corner and drowse, whenever no new attack of sickness forces me to offer a sacrifice to the water gods. I can rest for eight hours now—unless one of the peons or the ordinary seamen gets it into his head to harass me and make a joke out of my sickness. But I'm still hoping to escape their notice; perhaps I've found in Diego and García something in the way of protectors. At least they're not unfriendly to me. That could be helpful.

And then, toward evening, the second stage of the ordeal begins—the one when you wish you were dead. It starts with the wind swinging around. Before, the winds were blowing from the opposite direction, and the crew had turned the yards of the rectangular sail wide enough to sail to the wind. But now, toward evening, we get the real push to move.

Hanging at the stern of the flagship (and also on the caravels, I learn later) is an iron basin, which makes it possible to send messages or commands from ship to ship with smoke signals.

Diego knows all about it, which woods you have to use and how damp they have to be to produce the right volume of smoke in the daytime or the right fire at night. These signal fires are called *fumos* or *fuegos*, and both officers and men know their sequence or combination exactly. You can signal whether to change course, decrease or add sail, or approach the flagship to receive verbal orders.

In my miserable condition I only take in that Diego and a sailor are busy at the fire basin and don't struggle too hard to figure out why. I'm in no position to do that. Then orders are shouted, and the crew runs to the shrouds. I hear the singsong of the sailors, the creaking of the blocks, and suddenly the sounds of the ship change—the rhythm is different, new sounds are mixed in. The ropes seem to moan, the great linen sheets of the sails rattle like shots. Hissing, the bow wave lifts before the prow. We're making speed before the wind with full sail.

We shoot into valleys of waves, then rise onto house-tall peaks, racing into them as if we were driven by demons. I close my eyes in horror. What have I let myself in for? My teeth are chattering with fear. How can men give themselves to such a watery grave? How can they voluntarily declare themselves ready to leave firm land and undergo these dangers? I'm clinging to a rope with both hands. I may be washed overboard at any moment. Water sloshes over the deck. A wave sprays me in the face, blinds me, burns my eyes. It tastes repellently salty.

And then I hear someone praying beside me. Not the

Christian Our Father, but our Jewish prayer. *"Shema yisrael, adonai elohenu, adonai echod,"* murmurs a hoarse voice over me, at the mast where I am clinging, cowering. I take one hand from the rope, wipe my eyes, and blink up at the praying man. Right next to me, his hands clutching the wood of the mast, stands the man García had pointed out to me a while ago as the interpreter, his face greenish pale under his black hair. With eyes closed he murmurs the Hebrew words, "Hear, O Israel, the Lord is our God, the Lord is one—" Suddenly he feels I'm watching him. He quickly turns his head; our eyes meet. He breaks off the prayer, hastily mumbles a few crumbs of Latin, and crosses himself ostentatiously. Fear of discovery has made him even paler than he already was.

And I now know that there are three of us on board this ship that bears the most Christian name of all, the name of Mary, the Blessed Virgin. The ship's doctor from Moguer, denounced by one of the ship's boys. Now this interpreter, too. And I.

Chapter Three

*T*he way the Spanish see it, there are two kinds of baptized Jews: Conversos and Marranos.

Conversos, they say, are any Jews who have honestly converted to Christianity. A hundred years ago, something like that was still thought possible. They have become rich and respected Castilian families, and there are Conversos as ministers and financial advisors at the court of Their Most Christian Majesties Isabella and Ferdinand. People like the great Santángel, the man who made Columbus's expedition possible—as I learned on my flight after the bloodbath at Córdoba. But being rich and respected is of very little use to you in Spain today. As a Converso you lack something essential: a certificate from the Holy Inquisition that you are from an old Christian family and that your blood has been mixed with that of neither Moors nor Jews. Such a paper is called a *limpieza de sangre*—purity of blood. What it has to do with blood I don't know. I've seen Jewish blood flow during this last half year. It was red and looked no different at all from the blood of the Christians. Even such a powerful Converso as Luis de Santángel, for instance, for all his influence and his gold and his relationships, needed a royal letter of protection to put him beyond the grasp of the Inquisition and keep him from the stake.

For since the Inquisition was established, suddenly there are no more real Conversos in Spain. The Inquisition has decided that fundamentally all Conversos are Marranos.

Marrano is translatable. It simply means "swine." A Marrano is a Converso who merely appears to have turned to Christianity, someone who out of fear of the stake or even just to retain possession of his house and his fields has formally undergone the semblance of baptism but has really remained a Jew.

So however skillfully one of them can play the part, recite the Paternoster and the Ave Maria and name all the saints in his sleep, go to Mass every morning, and cross himself until his arm is sore—the Inquisition will find out anyway that he's a liar. They have the help of all his neighbors who do have the purity of blood. They all pay minute attention to whether the family of Conversos fasts on Fridays, whether the woman of the house also prepares pork, as is proper, and braises meat in milk.

They also don't hesitate to see if there's smoke rising from the chimney on Saturday and even put their hands on the wall behind the stove to see if it's warm. For that's how you can best recognize a Marrano: He of course plays at being a Christian, but he can't let go of the Jewish rituals. He doesn't eat fish on Fridays, pork remains an abomination to him, he never cooks meat and dairy in the same dishes, and of course he also doesn't cook on the Sabbath, in order not to profane the holy day. And so then they have him, the Converso who is really a Marrano, and throw him in prison or burn him at the stake.

Not that all this goes through my head as I'm crouching there behind the mast, battling against the retching in my throat, my stomach nerves quaking. At the moment I'm not up to it. I simply know—and how I know!—the fears that arise in a man who's just recently had himself baptized in order to make this journey and who can now be exposed as a Marrano by a ship's boy whenever he wants to. Of course, there are no priests on this ship, but there is a senior police officer to receive a denunciation. We're still not on the open sea. I've heard we're probably going to sail to islands far from the coast to take on fresh water and meat. And even if the journey is to the distant Indies, a disguised Jew isn't safe from derision, scorn, harassment—he may even have to fear for his life. A man is soon overboard if the others can't stand him.

And I can't do anything to dispel this interpreter's fears. I'd betray myself. All I can do is play dumb. So I stare straight ahead, swallow hard, belch and gag, and drag myself, staggering, to the railing, as if seasickness has driven understanding out of my head, and it's not at all hard for me, for if I'm pretending at first, my stomach also plays right along.

It's growing dark. Somehow I fall asleep right where I'm lying, with the knowledge that I have an enemy on this ship. One who fears me and therefore will try to harm me.

AGAIN THE SHIP'S BELL AWAKENS ME, and this time it no longer frightens me because I know it now, and again shortly afterward there's a sturdy kick in the ribs from my Alonso. Actually, in him I have yet another enemy on board.

"Get up, you vomiting landlubber! Your watch! Make room for a real seaman, you sissy!"

I stagger up. It's black night. I'm better, except that I feel as limp as a wrung-out handkerchief and my head aches unbearably. The big sail is rustling and rattling over me. The ship is still making full speed—which I actually get to feel when a swing of the *Santa María* knocks me back onto the deck, to shouts of laughter from the men around me. "Hang on, youngster!" I work my way aft hand over hand, from rope to spar, to reach the dimly glowing fire of the galley, where García sleeps, and

Diego, who is always—or is again—at his post and offers me his *bojito* with the water-wine mixture. My throat is parched. I swallow, and then I allow myself to chew and swallow a few bites of the *vizcocho*. I don't want to burden my quivering stomach with anything else.

During the meager meal, I look around me, and my fear returns. The sky is cloudy. On the stern I see the *fuego*, the glimmering firelight, dancing up and down like the torch in a Mardi Gras procession in Córdoba. The foam-crowned bow wave, hissing, breaks on both sides of the ship as our keel plows through the sea. Farther out I make out the fires of the *Pinta* and the *Niña*. They leap around like will-o'-the-wisps, disappear when they sink into a wave trough, reappear, and again make me aware of how the *Santa María* is also moving through the water. But this time I control my rebellious stomach, concentrate only on this, my ship. Everything is scary enough here anyway: billows that rise unexpectedly high along the lee railing, water that sprays on the deck, and if I look back, lights that appear to hop on the sea. It's as if there's light from the inside.

I am afraid. But I see that the others clearly find nothing at all unusual, and I take courage and get control of myself. For the first time I can even be glad that I'm feeling a little better again. Exhaustion spreads through my limbs. Diego, the friendly *despensero*, certainly meant well with the wine in the drink. But I have to pull myself together. After all, I have watch.

Furthermore, I feel I simply cannot postpone a certain matter any longer. I have of course kept almost no food and drink down for about twenty-four hours, and so I must be completely dehydrated. But it's no good. There's no help for it. My eyes search out the two "necessaries" in the darkness, roofed-over boards with a hole in the middle for sitting on, which are hung over the side. Luckily it's dark. I must see to it that I always manage to go there in the dark, for I recollect the other Pedro and Alonso telling of the marvelous jokes they play on the ship, especially when there are famous passengers: They hang on a rope over the side of the ship and watch the rear end of the lord prelate or admiral while he crouches there. I'm the opposite of a famous passenger. But does that rule out their having the same sort of fun with me?

All goes well, but when the ship heels I'm dipped up to the hips in water. Luckily the long-sleeved linen shirt that I wear, like almost everyone here on board, reaches halfway down my thighs. The salty dampness makes my skin burn.

The red-haired Basque mate, Chachu, who's in charge on this watch, comes up to me. "So, all crapped out? Then get to the ropes. And furthermore, how come you're running around like that? Why aren't you belted?"

I blink in confusion. Alonso, who's already curled up in my sleeping place, still has to put in his two cents and says maliciously, "That's the admiral's pet boy. He thinks he doesn't have to get his hands dirty."

The admiral? He's certainly forgotten me.

I take a breath to reply, but Chachu says curtly, "There're no lapdogs on this voyage; we have no room and no feed for those. Put some rope around you. You have to work in the shrouds."

Some rope? For the first time I notice that all these seafolk, unless they're part of the command, have belted their shirts with one or several ropes, some shorter, some longer. And I also understand immediately that it's very useful. You have what you need handy when something needs fixing, lashing, raising, or lowering, and if you know how to, you can secure yourself with it when you have to work in the rigging up on the mast. At least I'm well prepared for that. During my waiting time in Palos I had someone show me the knots. I only hope I remember the right one at the right time and don't fly off the top down to the water or, even worse, onto the deck.

But this time it doesn't come to that. I simply have to toil on the sails here below with the others, three, four, sometimes five of my watch.

It's lucky there are people who understand the commands. I'm not one of them. I hear a chaotic bellowing and can't make out anything at all—and if I could, I probably still wouldn't have any idea what it was about. But these seamen, most of them Basques, who know their bosun well, aren't depending on me. They're masters of their work, and I only have to do it along with them. And that seems to me hard enough.

The darkness seems impenetrable. A few horn lanterns illuminate the deck palely and show us where we are. But these men could probably do their work with their eyes closed. Cursing, we stagger around the deck, bump into each other in the dark, call each other names, and hang on tight when the ship sinks into a wave trough and then plunges up again; and not only I but others, too, run to the railing to vomit.

Our shirts snap in the stiff wind like the sails. They are damp and stiff with salt water—not just mine after my visit to the necessary. At some point each one has encountered his breaker. We nearly haul our hearts out, all together, and my heart is beating fit to burst. In a short time my palms are scoured raw, and the salt on them burns like fire. I feel as if I have no more skin left on my hands. But the others are also moaning and blowing on their hands.

Two, three times I slide and fall headlong, until someone shouts at me, "Numbskull, pitch the sandals over the side, for God's sake. There are only bare feet on the ship." He's right. However, I'm spared pitching them overboard. A surging wave takes care of that for me.

Whenever we've carried out a maneuver, we sink right down where we are, breathing hard, throats dry, and drift into a kind of half sleep until the next order gets us moving again. It's hellish. In between times I have to keep remembering to turn my sandglass. But that's also a certain consolation to me. That way I know just how much time has passed, and when I finally call out the next-to-last turn of the sandglass in a trembling voice that is lost in the wind, my eyes fill with tears of exhaustion and relief. Only half an hour more! Then this night's watch is over.

I can sleep. I don't care where.

IT WAS A MISTAKE. It was a terrible mistake. I ought to have known that the dreams come if I fall asleep without having armored myself against them in my thoughts, without having erected the wall to protect my soul, with a prayer, with reciting texts, with figuring, or just with counting. So I sink into sleep from exhaustion, but only my body is tired. In my head there begin the dreadful pictures of the things I've experienced. The pictures are like snakes in a pit. If you don't keep watch, they rear their heads over the edge. As a rule, I guard them well and send my thoughts along the dangerous edge like a sentry on patrol. But this time I haven't kept watch.

Most of all I fear two dreams that always return. Often the one changes into the other. Before I learned how to protect myself from them, they came to me every night after—after I left Córdoba and was on the open road.

At first a cold draft touches the back of my neck, and I know that someone who doesn't belong there has entered the gallery of our house. I stand in my room in the dark, holding my breath, the hair on my head standing up in terror. I know in this dream that I am the last and only one in the whole *judería,* the Jewish quarter, they haven't found yet. All the others have been hunted down and brought out. There is a pit in which there is fire. They are all standing together in the pit, pressed tightly against one another, and screaming prayers to God. I know that it is my duty to join in this prayer. But I also know that they will find me as soon as I raise my voice.

They are very close to me. I feel their hostile presence, the way you sense the presence of a predatory monster even if you don't see it. A scream grows in my throat, a scream that is also the prayer.

And with this scream I wake up and sit there with racing heart—when I dream only the one dream. But it can also continue. Then I hear someone calling from far away, *"Esther! Esther, querida, mi luz!"* And the voice that so tenderly calls me "Esther dear, my light" belongs to my *dueña,* Marta, Marta the Christian, who brought me up after the death of my mother and comforted me and refused to the end to leave our "unclean" house, even when it was already forbidden by decree for Christians to serve a Jewish master—because they might, it was said, be infected with the poison of heresy there.

In this second dream I am hugely relieved, for I know that now Marta will chase away the mob that has slipped in with the cold draft through our gallery, the way she used to chase from my room the great night moths that circled around the oil lamp and that I so feared. Marta, who with raised head, my hand in hers, passed the bunch of Christian riffraff who showered us with abuse. Marta, with whom you needn't be afraid.

I hear her steps on the stairs and leave my hiding place to run to meet her. . . . And then it is Marta, but she has no power to protect me.

The day after they took my father into the Casa Santa, the house of the Inquisition, under the deadly suspicion of murder and religious crimes, we found Marta on our doorstep in the morning. She was still breathing. There's little blood when they stone a person. Not, anyhow, the streams that flow when they hack someone's hand off with an axe, as happened to our house servant Laban because he'd raised it against a Christian (trying to ward off a blow that was aimed at my father). Anyway, Marta had only a thin stream of blood at the corner of her mouth. But her face was no longer recognizable at all. Everything was broken and cut, swollen and bruised, as if they'd not only thrown stones at her but had laid her head between two grinding millstones.

She died there in the house.

And in my dream, this Marta—whose face no longer exists, her bones broken, her limbs disjointed, covered with filth and blood—comes up the stairs to me and calls me: "*Esther, querida, mi luz!*"

At this point I usually wake up, and it's terrible enough. But tonight, on this ship, something new is added. For it is not Marta calling me but another voice—that of my father.

With a feeling of transcendent happiness, I leave my hiding place and rush to him. Yes, it is he, unchanged, as I last saw him in our house before they took him away, his good, olive-brown face, the eyes dark and glowing with wisdom and kindness, his neat beard and sidelocks. I want to kiss him and am rising on tiptoes toward him when I see that the tips of his beard are curling and smoking. And then the little tongues of fire shoot out of his hair and lick high at his face, this face whose skin in utter stillness blisters and draws together and explodes and shrinks to a black surface and is like a piece of charcoal, out of which a few teeth gleam, and then I am awake, the sweat running down my temples in streams and my hands curled out in a kind of convulsion. But obviously I have not screamed. Luckily I have not screamed. The soundlessness of the dream was the sign that at the last moment my head suppressed my fears, that I have not betrayed myself.

My teeth are chattering loudly. Dear God, watch over me! Give me strength to protect myself. *Cobre ánimo, Esther.* Be brave.

IT IS DEEP NIGHT, and I am on a ship. And something like this must never happen to me again. No dreams, Esther. Pedro, no dreams. Dreams are life-threatening. If I dream something like that again, something that leads

43

me and my spirit so close to the pit of oblivion, then everything will be futile. Then I can just throw myself right into the sea, for no one can live with that.

So. And now you will sleep again, Pedro, and forget all this. You will waste no second of your precious sleep. You will carefully guard the pit of snakes. We are not going there. Not to Córdoba, not into that house, not to those people. We are on our way in another direction. We are traveling into the unknown, with the man who has ocean eyes, and God has saved me.

And I try to bury the old, bad pictures deep and hang new ones in their place. But the new pictures aren't ready yet. Their outlines are blurred and fleeting, they keep changing, and they are also not ones to reassure me.

There was once, in my old life, a skillful gardener. His name was Efraim. Efraim had mastered the art of grafting onto an apple tree with sour, woody fruit a scion from another tree that bore better fruit, and the following year the bad tree would take on the habit of the good scion and bear juicy fruit. Efraim learned it from the Moors. He could also take an injured tree that threatened to die and at the proper time attach a piece of bark from another tree, and it would grow so firm that no one could see that it had ever been something alien. I wish such a healing bandage could be laid on my wounds and grow there and save me. Perhaps the man with the ocean eyes is this gardener.

To get to sleep again, I repeat a song to myself that

they sang in our *judería*. It is in Ladino, that remarkable mixture of Castilian, Hebrew, and Arabic that the simple folk use and we, the educated, scorn slightly. It tells of our ancestor Abraham. *Vido una luz santa en la giuderia que havia de nacer Avraham avinu*—he saw a holy light over Jewry that marked the birth of our father Abraham.

The song also exists as a Christian Christmas carol, to the same melody and with only a few words changed. But it comes from us.

Now I sleep. Without dreams this time. Can I ever be without fear again—fear awake, fear of sleeping?

THIS TIME IT'S THE BURNING PAIN in my hands that wakes me. Not only are my palms raw, but the nail beds and the skin between my fingers are swollen and inflamed from the salt water. I lift my arms over my head to let the wind cool them, and sit up. It's still dark. The ship is now moving along more smoothly, and this is also a quieter watch. Most men appear to be sleeping, except for the steersman, the lookout, and the officer in charge. A peon is dozing at the sandglass. Life on the *Santa María* seems to have settled into something like normal; apparently everyone knows what to do now, after the confusion and hecticness of the first day.

I stand up carefully. My stomach appears to have quieted, and I try to match the movements of the ship with my body, just so I don't need to use my torn hands to hang on to anything.

Aft, on the poop deck, sits the *toldilla,* the cabin. The quarters of Admiral Columbus. A beam of light comes from the tiny window. The admiral! I haven't given any more thought to him in the tribulations of the last couple of days, what with seasickness, the watch, and everything else. He was only present in my sleep. Is he still up at this hour between night and day, this ghost watch, when sleep closes a man's eyes and makes him heavy as a sack of sand? I'm quite certain he's forgotten me. It wouldn't be surprising. But I've looked into his eyes, and that remarkable feeling that I got then is suddenly here again. And can it not also be that I'll need him and his help on this ship, supposing he even wants to give it to me at all?

The pains in my hands are forgotten. Careful not to stumble over a coil of rope or a reserve spar, I feel my way with my bare feet to the raised afterdeck.

The admiral's *toldilla* is built over a cabin in which, I've heard, the noble passengers are supposed to be lodged. But when I see how tiny this cabin over them is, I cannot imagine how those three or even four men are crowded together into so small a space. Everything is quiet. I can't resist the temptation to go up to the window, stand on tiptoe, and peer in.

There's an oil lamp burning on the table. Behind it I see the closed curtains of a bed—surely the only bed on the ship. There's also an iron-bound seaman's trunk and another, smaller one, almost like a strongbox. Certainly maps and papers must be kept in it. The table is covered with a linen cloth. An inkwell sits on it, along with a book and two nautical instruments that I've never seen before. And a compass, that I know, the disk with thirty-two divisions on a scale. Just like the steering compass beside the rudder shaft and the big one in the binnacle, the little compass house outside under its rain bonnet. This one, too, is fastened to a kind of cone, so that it can turn with the movement of the ship. I can see the needle trembling.

No sign of the admiral. He's probably sleeping.

"No, the admiral is not sleeping. God gives a man He sends on such a journey the power to remain awake longer than the mass of ordinary mortals."

His voice with its unfamiliar Genoese accent, as gentle as it may be, strikes me like a whiplash. What shadow has he emerged from? He's surprised me as I was intending to spy on him. I feel my cheeks begin to flame.

"Were it not so dark, Your Grace could see my embarrassment," I say after a little pause in which I pull myself together.

He laughs softly. They say he laughs very seldom—never, really. My confusion grows. "You know how to express yourself, Pedro," he replies. "There's nothing for which you need excuse yourself. I've been expecting you. After all, you are on this ship through me and for me." What he says is simple, but it sounds so remarkably mysterious and laden with significance that I have the feeling he's going to honor me with an important communication.

"Now, come with me," he continues. "I want to show you something."

He turns and goes ahead of me to the aftercastle, a tall, dark form on light feet, the wind playing with his white hair. I notice that he isn't wearing his beret. Perhaps it pleases him to expose his face to the salty spray and let it dry again in the cool movement of the air.

"Here," he says, stopping so suddenly that I almost crash into him. He lifts his hand and points forward.

And all at once I'm able to see with his eyes. It's like a spell.

The glowing bow wave, fraught with danger, rolls from the center and piles up on both sides of the ship like a wall—it no longer looks like a threat to me. It seems to me as if the Lord is parting the waves before us so that we can pass through, as He did for my ancestors on their journey through the Red Sea when they left Egypt for freedom. For freedom! The keel plows its way through the watery element, swift as an arrow, forward, ever forward! The snapping and cracking of the wind-filled sails, the groaning of the rudder, and the taut ropes with the wind singing through them, the quick shudder and echoes that seem to run along the deck—it is a universe of movements and powers. And behind me is the man who knows these powers and masters them.

I feel his presence behind me. It's as if he emits a current. I sense that he is happy here in this place, here on board this ship. Why is he letting me share this feeling with him? I am exalted as the *Santa María* climbs the waves. Why me?

I dare to turn around to him, with an indescribable mixture of anxiety and fascination. But he isn't looking at me. His gaze is directed forward in the dimly gleaming darkness.

"I was like one who carried his wings in his hands and had a stone at his feet." Did he really say that? And to me?

"How fast we are," I murmur, to counteract his spellbinding. For I want no spellbinding. I'm afraid of anything like that. Where might it carry me? I've escaped, that's enough. Feelings are traitors. They make you weak.

He replies, without changing his tone or posture, "The *Santa María* is not a fast ship. The Pinzóns' caravels are much faster. But we're making good time now. Fifteen leagues since we've been on the open sea."

His hair blows in the wind. His face seems alight.

Fifteen leagues ... how does he know that so precisely? When were the measurements taken on this ship, where just a little while ago everything was at sixes and sevens?

"How did Your Grace determine that?" I ask. I ask it carefully, almost reverently. Instinctively I feel that I mustn't show him any mistrust or doubt his authority. And I think they've certainly been doing that for a long time at court. Certainly people have shaken their heads over his plans . . . to the Indies! Ha . . . They laughed at him, in the committees and in the bars in the port cities, as in Palos, where they called him Don Fantástico.

"I see it in the waves," he answers simply. "By the time it takes the wave crests to get from bow to stern."

"Do you measure the time?"

"I don't have to measure it. I see it."

I translate his words to myself. He estimates it, then. Beside the half-hour glass hangs a piece of wood weighted with lead, which has a line attached that is subdivided by a series of knots at regular intervals. This is a *corredera,* a log chip. They throw it into the water, and depending on the number of the knots running out, they measure the speed the ship is making. But our *corredera* is not in the water.

"And how do you know where the ship is?" I ask again, eager and anxious at the same time. I'm becoming aware that I want less to know about the voyage than to know about this voyager, Christopher Columbus, the man who is standing behind me and speaking with such a soft voice.

"The stars and the compass guide the master mariner," he replies. It sounds like a theorem. I look up at the cloudy sky, and he sees my movement and continues, "But when we sail into unknown waters, the stars are no longer useful to us. Their pictures change the farther we go, where no man has ever been yet. So there's only the needle of the compass and God the Almighty."

I know that the man standing behind me now makes the sign of the cross, as is the custom in Spain at the mention of the highest being, and that I have to do it, too. Nevertheless, I do not do it, and I also know that he notices.

"May the Lord be with Your Grace's spirit," I say instead. I feel indescribable. I'm afraid and I'm fascinated. I'm not myself anymore. What is it emanating from this tall form that I am so aware of behind me?

"Come to my cabin," he says. "I want to show you something."

Chapter Four

"I expect you, as my page and helper, to give me a hand with the entries into the logbook," says Columbus.

It's hot and sticky in the *toldilla*. The cooling brought by the night and the wind hasn't reached the inside of this wooden box. The admiral takes off his cloak and holds it out to me on his outstretched arm, and I understand that I'm supposed to fold the garment and probably put it in the chest, but when I open the lid, he says, "No. Put it on the bed."

He isn't looking at me. And in what follows, he never looks at me directly, either, but nevertheless he's obviously observing me the whole time.

Without his luxurious cloak he looks slender and tall. The muscles of his shoulders and back appear powerful under the white shirt with the full sleeves. A seafarer, a man who has done what others on the ship do now, who has served from the bottom, who has torn his hands like mine and toiled his heart out, who—

Stop. What happened to my nausea? It's as though it has blown away. And since I've been talking with him, I no longer feel the pain in my hands. It returns now, of course, worse than before. That's because in the lamp-light I can see for the first time how bad my hands are. Red and puffy from salt water, the palms raw and bloody from the work on the ropes.

"That will pass," he says, as if he's read my thoughts. "Look here. These are the instruments." He points to the two devices I saw through the window of the *toldilla*. The first is a kind of metal dish with embossed geometric figures. The second is a quarter circle made of wood with two holes along one side. From the tip of the instrument there hangs a plumb bob.

"This," says the admiral, pointing to the first one, "is an astrolabe. Ptolemy, the Greek, invented it to measure the angles of the stars in relation to each other and so determine their height. It's a tool for astronomers, not for sailors. Only the learned can use it. The second is called a quadrant. With its help one can, when the sea is calm, take a bearing on the pole star and thus determine where one is. I can make you familiar with it, Pedro, in a calm or on land—we'll be sailing to the islands before we voyage on to the Indies."

He says it so matter-of-factly that a shiver runs through me—as if he'd already been there!

"Could Your Grace also teach me how to use the astrolabe?" I ask, just to say anything at all.

"No," he replies calmly. "I'm no mathematician. I'm a seaman. I have no idea how to use it. It's only there on the table to impress the ignorant minds on this ship. It's supposed to strengthen their faith in me."

I gulp. "But the quadrant?"

"It is of little use. However, it can be helpful on occasion."

During this speech he's pulled out a key that he's wearing on a chain around his neck, along with a crucifix. He takes it off the chain and uses it to open the metal-bound casket, in whose lock is stuck another key. As he does so, he places himself so that I can't see the contents of this chest. He removes a roll of papers held together with wooden fasteners into a notebook, a bundle of feathered quills, and a small knife. "Sharpen the quills, Pedro," he instructs me.

I take a place at the table, in front of the inkwell, which is corked and fastened to the edge of the table with clips, and for a moment I feel sick. Sitting down, I feel the motion of the ship more strongly, and when I grasp the feathers and the knife, I'm aware that my hands are swollen, injured clods, unwieldy and unable to carry out fine tasks. But that's only the first reason. The other is that it is a task from the past, a task from the time that I must forget with all my power in order to be able to live on now in the present. I clench my teeth and swallow hard. It doesn't work. I must tell him that it won't work. I hold my hands out to him as if they didn't belong to me. Helplessly I turn my head away from him, but he's walked up behind me again, as he stood behind me on the poop deck. I hear the soft clicking of the beads of his rosary sliding through his fingers. (His hands are constantly in motion; he's always doing something.)

"Sharpen the quills, Pedro," he repeats sternly. "Then open the ink bottle and write what I dictate to you."

Of course he sees how things are with me. He simply doesn't let it matter. With difficulty I carry out his orders. I feel like a cow being instructed in sewing, my hands are so clumsy with the pain. But I manage. Somehow I manage.

I dip the quill, scrape off the extra ink on the edge of the bottle, draw the paper toward me, and wait, hand poised, for his dictation. Then suddenly I feel that he has turned away from me, and a searing fear shoots through me—but his action has nothing at all to do with me. "What's that? What does this mean? Do you feel it, too?" he asks hurriedly. I feel nothing at all except the racing of my heart, but he tears open the door of the *toldilla*, and I hear him cursing in Italian: "*Gentaglia ignorante! Fatto male! Corpo di Bacco!* Who's the steersman? Pilot! Can't you keep on course, you bungler? Is this what sailing to the wind means?"

Hurrying feet patter over the deck. The drowsy ghost watch turns into hectic activity, the bosun's whistle shrilling, commands being bellowed. Indeed, now even I notice what he must have felt: The *Santa María* has slowed her speed, her movements are different, her song has changed. The steersman probably nodded off. The sails flap in the wind, and I give thanks to heaven for making that drowsiness come over the man at the tiller. For at that very moment I'd just placed my hand with the quill at the right side of the page instead of at the left, the way I always did when taking dictation from my father. I was about to write Hebrew script instead of Latin. The *Santa María*'s going off course has apparently saved me from being found out.

He comes back in again. His usually pale face is red with anger, and he sends the rosary circling through his fingers in a not very submissive manner, but his voice already sounds calm again when he says to me, "Begin now, Pedro. Write: In the name of God. I have resolved to write down, day by day, most conscientiously, what occurs on this voyage . . ."

IT HAS GROWN LIGHT. I don't know how it happened. I'm so awake that I might never have to sleep again. The watches have changed outside. The *despensero*, Diego, has come and without being asked has brought water, *vizcocho*, dried fruit, and olives for the admiral, and Don

Cristóbal has told him that his page is no longer to do any service at all on the ship.

Diego nods and casts me a look I'm unable to figure out. Is it goodwill, surprise, disapproval? It may be important for me to know which, but other things concern me at the moment.

The man with whom I'm sitting here at the table, bending over a sea chart of the waters along the coast of Spain, appears to know no weariness. With compass and ruler he draws the course and distances covered on two maps. Why two? Before my eyes, without measuring or adjusting, he's drawn the existing chart. On a second sheet, with one continuous line, no stopping, no correcting, there arise the contours of the Spanish and Portuguese coasts and the islands in the ocean beyond—Canaries, Azores, Cape Verde. I've never seen anything like it. With the remarkable certainty of a migratory bird flying straight to its goal, the feathered quill in his hand draws the way, clearly, evenly, completely. It takes my breath away.

"So," he says. "Now we have two charts." (Meanwhile he puts in the cities and the harbors and labels the islands.) "I will now enter in the secret chart where we really are."

"Where we are? How have you arrived at that, Don Cristóbal?"

"You don't need to learn that, Pedro," he says coolly.

"It's enough if you are able to enter the information I give you on these charts."

"Is it a secret?" I ask.

"It's an art," he replies, toying with the knife. His movements are sure and quiet. "It's known as dead reckoning. I determine it with the help of the ship's speed, the direction and force of the wind, the drift I observe, the compass, and the stars. I know the sea. The sea and I, we work together."

These words seem to call for a smile. But his expression doesn't alter.

"Now, take your chart," he orders. "You saw how I did it, didn't you? You will now draw the chart that is intended for the others."

"How does Your Grace mean?"

"Just do what I tell you. Put in up here ten leagues. Not fifteen. Place the compass so. Make the circle smaller. Put the tangents farther toward southsouthwest. That's good."

Numbly I follow his instructions. So I am forging the sea chart.

"Will Your Grace permit a question as to why this is happening?" I murmur.

"Good sea charts should be secrets," he replies, as if it were a self-evident truth. "One keeps them to oneself."

"But won't the other captains also take measurements and make calculations?"

"Certainly they will do that. But in contrast to me,

they won't keep track of them. We'll probably argue about details, or even not. Also, sometimes I'll give them the right ones, and they'll forget them again. Only I will know the route we're sailing. It doesn't become important until we have the islands behind us, but it's better to begin now."

He talks about this deception as if it has to be this way. "Besides," he continues, "I must protect myself from that Basque."

He makes a motion of his head toward the foreship, and I understand he means the owner, Juan de la Cosa. "I leased this ship for seven hundred fifty leagues westward and back. But it will probably be longer to the Indies. He mustn't know that."

I stare at him openmouthed. What is running through my head is: Typical Genoese, the way they're described in books, cunning and sly. And my fear, this anxiety that pursues me constantly, is suddenly so overwhelming that I have to ask, "Why do you confide all these things in me, Don Cristóbal? Who am I, after all?"

The oceanic eyes are trained on me. "I do not believe that I can trust the fleet secretary," he says. "Besides him, you're the only one who understands Latin. Probably better than I, I suspect. You're intelligent. You learn quickly, as I observe. But you're only a grummet. In a serious situation, nobody would believe you. Furthermore, you're pretending to be something other than you are."

I feel gooseflesh on my arms. By the God of my fathers, what does he know? What do those eyes see?

A shadow falls over the table. "Is one permitted to enter?" asks a deep voice. An older man stands on the threshold, almost bald, his shoulders rounded, and he has a sailcloth bag in his hand.

"Of course. I sent for you, Maestro Bernal," says the admiral. "An old wound under my shoulder has been giving me pain since yesterday. Please take a look at it. And you, Pedro, have spilled some ink, fortunately only on the tablecloth and not on the chart. Take the cloth off. We won't need it on this voyage anyway."

While I follow his orders, still stunned by what he just said to me, he removes his shirt. I turn away, and the older man busies himself with things from his bag. So this is the ship's doctor, the one the boys claimed is a Marrano from Moguer.

"It's nothing, Your Grace," he observes now, "or as good as nothing. Maybe the weather. In any case, there's no inflammation to be seen."

"But I still feel it," the admiral insists.

"One sometimes feels things that aren't there."

"I can understand that. And there are other things there that no one feels. No, let it be, *maestro*. No salves if it really is nothing. How's the condition of the crew?"

"They're just bursting with health—if one doesn't consider such trivialities as seasickness. Your doctor is going to be bored on the voyage."

"That would be good. Oh, and while you're here—take care of the boy's hands. It hinders his waiting on me and writing for me. You're dismissed, Pedro. I'll have you called."

MY RETURN TRIP from the admiral's *toldilla* to the deck of the ship is not exactly a triumphal march. Hateful looks and malicious remarks come from all sides. There's no thought of following the admiral's orders and releasing me from duty on the ship. First of all a pail and a gorse broom are pressed into my hands, although I don't have watch. I have to wash and scrub the deck—in the heat the planks shrink easily, and there are cracks and splits. Naturally my salve-covered hands become an occasion for gibes. "Did Don Fantástico put salve on his poor little lapdog's paws?" the peons jeer.

I keep quiet and do the work they give me, though I feel weak and dizzy. I've hardly slept and have eaten nothing for half an eternity—the admiral didn't offer me any of the things on his table, and anyway, I was too excited and busy to feel my hunger. Now my martyred stomach is cramping with hunger. Change of watch is past, so there'll be nothing until noon.

In a free moment I discover that my bundle has been ransacked. I thank heaven that I buried my father's phylacteries before I came on the ship. There's nothing suspicious they could have discovered. There are only a pair of old trousers and my second shirt, the worn-out sash to belt it—now taken care of by the rope around my waist—a wooden comb, and a knife so dull and nicked that they didn't even consider it worth stealing. My money belt doesn't have a single maravedi left in it. They all went to the ship's secretary.

I tie the things up again and give the bundle a scornful kick. It doesn't matter if I have it or not.

"Did someone rob you?" one of the sailors asks me. "It was sure to be the Basques. All Basques are thievish folk."

"No one stole anything from me, because there's nothing to steal," I answer.

"Yes, well, all the same. Don't hang around with the Basques so much. You're an Andalusian, aren't you? Andalusians should stick together."

I shrug. I don't see the tiniest reason that should drive me over to the Andalusians, to Alonso and his pals. The Basques are friendly to me.

"I think the shipowner is also a Basque?" I inquire.

"Not just him!" confides my shipmate. He lowers his voice. "The whole thing is a conspiracy of Basques and other foreigners. If we don't watch out, they'll tip us all overboard some night."

"Why would they do that?"

"They just would. Because they're bastards. They want to get rid of us so they have the gold all to themselves."

It couldn't be more crackbrained. Andalusian delusions of persecution. "I don't understand," I say. "Then we wouldn't have crew enough. Then no one would get the work done, either."

"Right," says the fellow, as if I hadn't contradicted him at all. "We do all the work for them. And they want to pocket everything. Just wait. Someday they'll show their true faces. They all wear the same hat—Basques, Genoese, Venetians, Moors, Jews."

I've been expecting that.

"And where are they, the Moors and the Jews?" I ask challengingly.

"They'll show themselves yet. We'll hunt them out!" he says threateningly. I'm beginning to feel very uneasy. But luckily García calls to me.

"Hey, boy, if you're going to work anyway, even when it's not your turn, then give me a hand now. Bring me firewood and help me clean the beets."

"Don't let them bother you!" my Andalusian friend advises me again. But I'm glad to do something for García. He likes me, and as long as I'm doing something for him, the others can't ask me to. Besides, with my gigantic hunger, it's perfect for me to be sitting right there at the source.

But—new horror! Garcia is cooking the beets for today's meal with the pickled meat from the barrel. With pork.

This is what they've used to keep ferreting out the Conversos as Marranos, this pork. Jewish dietary laws state that the swine is an unclean animal. Therefore Jews loathe eating pork, even when they've converted to Christianity. It doesn't necessarily have anything to do with belief at all. It's simply a matter of living habits. No person in Spain, whether Muslim, Christian, or Jew, considers eating maggots or blowflies. They may possibly not even taste bad. And even if someone were to suddenly come along and preach, "Eat maggots, eat blowflies! They're delicacies and enrich the menu!" still nobody would be able to overcome their disgust from one day to the next. They're brought up that way. It's just exactly the same with pork. So they might have become Christian from the depths of their hearts and pray to the triune God—but they cannot swallow the meat of an unclean animal. And then it's: Aha, your Christianity is only a sham. Because there you are, still obeying the dietary laws of the Jews.

I'm no Conversa. I need never act as if I wanted to eat that food. I can't and don't want to. I am a Jew who keeps to the law. I know. Before the fall of Granada, when hunger was tormenting the Moors, they are even supposed to have devoured parts of corpses. But I'm not facing death by starvation, even though I am hungry. I won't eat any of this.

So I pretend to have a new attack of seasickness, and though the smell of the beet soup tickles my nostrils seductively, I act as if I were going to hang over the railing. I'll find a piece of *vizcocho* at the beginning of the next watch.

Chapter Five

The *fumos*, the smoke signals from the *Santa María*'s basin of coals, call the flotilla's two other ships to come closer for a captains' conference. We're still under full sail, and in the meantime I'm able to marvel at the utter ease with which the Pinzóns' two caravels maneuver up to our clumsy *nao*. The admiral, again wearing his red cloak, the beret on his white hair, stands up on the aftercastle, the speaking tube in his hand. The owners and the navigators, the pilots, take part in the conference. I note that not one of the crew, except maybe the mate, is interested in what's being discussed. Navigation and strategy are matters for the officers. They have nothing to do with the common man. He just carries out the orders.

However, I can hardly follow either. The wind carries

the voices away. Certainly someone who knew what it was about could make out a great deal, and I'm not one of those. But I do understand that the pilots of the *Pinta* and the *Niña* completely confirm Columbus's calculations about the speed—what did he call it? Estimate? No, reckoning, dead reckoning. They, however, have made use of the log chip, the *corredera*.

Then, if I understand correctly, they go on about the shape of the sail. The *Santa María* and the *Pinta* have big, square sails. The dainty little *Niña* uses the triangular sails they call lateens. The admiral wants the *Niña* to change its sheets when we get to the Canary Islands, and Captain Yáñez Pinzón is arguing with him. The caravel is nimbler and faster with the lateens.

"There are different winds ahead of us!" the commander intones through his speaking tube. "Just wait till we cross behind the islands! Your sails will be like a butterfly's wings in a thunderstorm!"

Then follow still more orders about the rigging, which the two caravel captains receive only with silence and sheepish faces. No comments and no arguments.

When the ships separate again to continue the voyage, the *Niña* flies away frolicsomely and elegantly, like a young girl doing the fandango, and the wind fills out her triangular sails as if they were maiden's chemises.

But then, once all the ships have taken their positions, everywhere the same commands are given, their sense clear to me only when they are carried out. The rigging is shortened, the upper sheets reefed almost to half-mast. With a hollow wailing, the wind hurls itself into the rigging; it rattles and whistles, the remaining sails receiving it with a crack, bellying like barrels. We're now moving differently, more jerkily, and also more slowly.

In the middle of all this the bells strike, and one of the peons bawls: "On deck, all good seamen of the duty gang! To your watch, master pilot's men. It's your turn now, be nimble about it."

This really is my watch now, and the first thing I do is to get myself to the sandglass to turn it, as is proper, thanking God in the silence as I go that I once again have missed having to climb the yards.

Beside me is one of the Basque sailors I already know, making one of the shrouds fast to a block. He's a little slow-witted, but he's not one of the rough ones.

"Do you know what all this means?" I ask, pointing aloft with my chin toward the empty tops of our masts.

"Hm," he growls, and pulls the lay tight. "I can at least guess."

That doesn't make me any wiser. But I gather I'm not the only one curious about this matter. The crew's mood is subdued, and from half hints I finally get the picture for myself.

The Portuguese! That's the unanimous opinion. Clearly, the admiral is afraid Portuguese ships might intercept us in these waters, so he's had the sail taken in so there will be less chance of our being seen on the horizon.

The speculation is confirmed when the best men with the sharpest eyes are sent up into the crow's nest to keep an eye on the northeast. That way, we'll be the first to see the Portuguese and can try to outrun them.

So, the Portuguese! It's true, there's no war going on between Spain and Portugal, only sort of a competition for control of markets and spheres of influence. But the contest for these is so intense that the Pope himself has intervened and has with his own hand, so to speak, drawn a line through the sea to separate Portuguese and Spanish waters. And even though we're now sailing in the Spanish area of the sea, it isn't at all rare for pirates on either side to intrude into the other's, prohibited, waters. Thus extreme caution and alertness are required. Especially since we're utterly unarmed, if you don't consider the bombardment that would let loose from land if they could see what was happening. One armed Portuguese fast yacht could annihilate this entire flotilla.

Lovely prospect! The question remains, why should they be so keen to catch us that we have to sneak along here slowly, cowering like a rabbit before a snake?

In a free moment I dare to ask García about it. His mouth stretches into a crooked grin.

"The Portuguese love our admiral more than anything," he says, pulling down his lower eyelid with one finger. "Don't you know he tried to get ships for this voyage to the Indies in Portugal first?'

"Yes, I know that," I reply, although it's not true, "but King John must not have believed him."

García nods. "Hm. Maybe he's sorry now. Maybe it's like the dog who doesn't want to chew on his bone until you call a bigger dog. If Their Majesties Ferdinand and Isabella take Señor Colón seriously, then there must be something in it. Could be. But also it could be something entirely different." After a significant pause, he continues in a lowered voice, "They say our admiral had to leave Lisbon in a big hurry. They were right on his heels. They say he helped himself to something His Majesty was very unhappy to lose. A state secret." Behind a hand held to his mouth, he whispers, "Señor Colón is supposed to have pocketed a copy of a secret sea chart from the Portuguese royal archives. And the noble gentlemen don't care at all for a thing like that to happen."

Now I can think about that while I go about my work.

It's true, sea charts are state secrets. At the same time, they're treasure maps, guides to a part of the world where there's something to find, and the faster and more precisely one steers there, the bigger the reward will be. Every captain tries to obscure his sailing charts, so very much that sometimes it's almost laughable. Any child knows that. Even the uneducated sailors on this ship know that. But a chart for the sake of which a royal fleet goes on an intercepting course? I dimly remember my father telling me of an Italian scholar named Toscanelli, who was supposed to have drawn a map of the world like that for Portugal. But I was a child then, and besides, I wasn't interested in maps, even if the antipodes were on them or the spice islands of the Arabian empire. My interest in geography, like that of many thousands of Jews, awakened only when it was a matter of finding countries for survival.

Toscanelli's world map. And Columbus saw it and copied it?

In any case, we now sail with extreme caution for an entire day, until the admiral cancels the alert and we raise full sails to the tops again. No one can explain to me how he knows the danger is past. They merely shrug and say, "He just knows the water."

By now the fine gentlemen passengers have apparently gotten over their seasickness. They come crawling out of their holes, still green in the face and on wobbly legs, standing at the railing with closed eyes and deeply inhaling the salty air. The man García tells me is a major-domo of Their Majesties' court, and who is probably a kind of servant for the *señores*, comes to Diego and demands this and that from him for the comfort of the fine folks. Diego takes pains to be polite. He pulls at his red wool cap, listens to the demands, and nods, but you can see that he's almost bursting with impatience.

I'm sitting next to García. My watch is over, I'm dead tired, and I'm gnawing on a piece of rock-hard flatbread with cheese. I feel protected with García. He appears to like me, and as long as I'm near him, none of the peons dares come near me. Now he makes observations about our fellow passengers while he stirs up his little fire and has me breaking up brushwood, for the gentlemen wish to dine. I listen carefully. Everything I know can be of use to me.

"Diego de Arana," García growls through his teeth, gesturing with his cooking spoon toward a man with a head of curly hair and a pockmarked face, "our *alguacil,* our police official for all the ships. He might be his own best customer, the way I see it. He's a procurer from Córdoba who sent his own cousin to the Genoese's bed. He got her a kid, and now Don Diego is allowed on the great voyage. A child sponsor, as they say. Oh, well, everyone provides for his family."

García mixes the rest of the beets with a new portion of pickled pork. The noble gentlemen get no special menu. They eat what's in the pot. And they didn't have to come. I wonder about the ship's doctor and the interpreter, how this food will appeal to them.

Meanwhile the cook continues his list. "That one there with the stiff collar—huh, how long'll they wear that stuff on the ship?—that's the *veedor real,* the royal comptroller, the clerk ordered aboard by Their Majesties so he can keep an eye on the treasure when we get there. Trust is good, supervision is better. Anyway, his name is Sánchez. Does that mean anything to you? Sánchez from Segovia. A relative of Luis de Santángel. And Santángel is the man who provides the nice little maravedis the admiral has used to rent these ships here, understand? On the orders of Their Majesties, of course. And the man doing the hiring is Luis de Santángel."

I've known that longer than he has. But nevertheless I'm impressed by how much gets talked about in the harbor taverns.

"That one there," García goes on, again gesturing with his stirring spoon, "is the fleet secretary, Señor Escobedo. He knows a thing or two. He'd take your last penny." I can confirm that. No one needs to tell me anything about Escobedo.

"And who's that tall one there?" I ask while I push the firewood to García stick by stick. He's clearly enjoying my going along with his game, grinning slyly at me. "That one's the great unknown. Don Misterioso," he says. "His name's Gutiérrez. Pedro, like you. Said to be traveling as a private person. Even supposed to have paid for his passage."

He's not the only one, I think. But García interrupts my thoughts, giving me a conspiratorial wink as he says, "If you ask me, he's one thing at the very least: eyes and ears for Isabella and Ferdinand. I'll bet my earring against a rotten sardine he's one of the Holy Brotherhood."

A cold feeling creeps down my spine. The Holy Brotherhood, Santa Hermandad—they're the spies of the

Inquisition, those who betray victims and drive them toward the spiritual lords, and for this they receive not only the promise of heavenly joys but cash payment while still on earth. Admittedly, in recent times it has seemed the Hermandad might be quite superfluous, for every good Spaniard of pure blood has taken over this work with pleasure. I know it was one of Santángel's conditions that no priests and no one of the Brotherhood was to go along on the voyage.

I try to remain calm. García is a simple sailor, and he certainly also gets things confused or believes in rumors. It's entirely possible that Their Majesties have sent along a personal informant or watchdog. But at the same time he doesn't necessarily have anything to do with the grand inquisitor, Torquemada...I simply must suppress these thoughts. There's enough for me to puzzle over here on board.

The matter of the possible Portuguese pursuit has loosened the men's tongues. It seems to all as if we've outrun a real danger, not merely a possible one, and now when their work gives them time, they chatter about what's in store for them.

I'm sitting with the Basques again; it's worked out that way because I've shared a watch with them, and besides, at the moment I find them much more agreeable than the Andalusians. At least I know that none of them has put my relatives in a kettle of boiling water or, in order to convert him, has taken a son away from his father and beaten him to death, as happened to my uncle and cousin. These Basque men were all either on long voyages during the last years or were up there in the north, in their own country. Besides, except for García and Diego, who are openly friendly toward me, they possess the admirable characteristic of simply taking no notice of me whatsoever. And since the shipowner is a Basque, the seamen from the south of the country are targets for their scorn.

"One of these Andalusian blockheads actually just said that the world is something like a soup plate and we're now sailing along the edge of the dish," remarks a round-faced fellow with a double chin and a typical northern accent, thus provoking the derogatory laughter of the Basque faction present. What ignorance! Any beginner knows, even if he's only been to sea once, that you first see the tips of the masts and the sails of strange ships on the horizon and then the body of the ship. Otherwise the admiral wouldn't have set sail at all. Clear case.

"Hm," says a younger man thoughtfully as he cuts a torn fingernail with his cutlass, "all the same, there's something I don't understand. How can a ship sail uphill?"

There is thoughtful silence for a moment. Then Chachu, the bosun, says superciliously, "Idiot! The wind pushes it uphill. The wind and the currents." This explanation appears to enlighten everyone. However, they sit there and ponder.

"Has any of you ever sailed out beyond the islands before the wind?" the younger one asks again.

"None of us," growls Chachu. "But ask them there!" He points with a thumb at a group of four men who have somehow managed always to have the same watch and who plainly keep themselves separate from the others. "They were personally hired on by the admiral, and it's said he has them from—well, let's leave it at that. I don't want to burn my mouth here. They're supposed to have sailed with him before. Out into the Green Sea of Darkness, out there in the West."

The Green Sea of Darkness. Where we, too, will soon be sailing. Not exactly a confidence-inspiring description. It produces uneasy silence. And no one seems to have any real desire to ask those four about anything. I can understand that. They don't exactly look as if they wanted to talk to anyone.

"Oh, well," says Double Chin finally, blowing his nose. "The Portuguese are also sailing around in that area."

"That's a great comfort," replies my friend García with a dry laugh. "To think we might possibly still meet those bounty chasers behind the Canaries as well! Besides, everyone knows the Portuguese only make a detour, so to speak, to get to Africa down below. They simply let that damned Sea of Darkness lie to the starboard, you understand! And sail south-southwest."

"We're also sailing south-southwest," someone else chimes in, and again there's an awkward silence.

A gray-headed man wearing a neckerchief of Moorish silk from which he's obviously never parted jumps in. "I'd like to have your worries!" His voice sounds irritated. "It's none of our business what course we're setting. That's for our master captains to do. The good Lord appointed them to do that. It's *their* job to get us there and back safely. *They* have to answer before God's judgment for the fate of their crew. If we begin to break *our* heads over it, then we'll go astray. Every man in his place, I always say! Whether south-southwest or northeast, it's all the same to me." He raises the *bojito* and lets the stream of water mixed with wine flow into his mouth.

"That's quite right!" García says soothingly. "However, if the fish eat me or the Portuguese hang me from the yards, it's no comfort to me if the admiral goes to hell for it."

The men laugh.

"No more about the fish and no more about the Portuguese," declares Chachu with energetic cheer. After all, as bosun, he's a kind of link between officers and men and has to keep up morale. "We'll be swimming in gold! Juan de la Cosa said so. And the Pinzóns, too. In general I don't think much of those folks from Palos and Moguer, but the Pinzóns have a nose for gold, that we can say. And the admiral has a nose for gold as well. All Genoese know how to feather their own nests. When we first get there—"

"Yes, *if* we first get there," the younger one suggests, and again the silence descends over the men.

"We have seven hundred fifty leagues in the contract," replies Chachu energetically. "And we won't sail a hands-breadth farther. Our shipowner will see to that. I know de la Cosa, I've been with him for years here on the *Gallega,* even if she is now called the *Santa María.* He won't let anybody put anything over on him."

"Well, good," says Double Chin. "Assuming everything works. We're there. We get more gold than we can carry. Wonderful. But how do we get back again?"

"What do you mean?" asks the younger one nervously.

"Every child knows the earth is no soup plate. It's something like a ball. Or like this apple here." He reaches over to García's provisions basket and takes an apple before García can stop him and then takes the cutlass from the boy who was just cleaning his nails with it and runs it along the skin of the apple. "So, now, look. If Spain is here—here we are. And now we're sailing down around here. And so on around. Always before the wind. Obviously we have good winds and water. We're going uphill. But back? Then we have to go against the wind and against the currents. How are we going to come up again?"

He cuts into the apple, divides it, and begins to eat it with smacking noises. I put my hand to my mouth to cover my smile, and then it occurs to me that this argument among the uneducated seamen—how can a ship sail uphill?—was also used by a congress of scholars at Salamanca, and the recollection rescues me from arrogance. How should they know? Naturally they want to come back again. Not, like me and possibly a few others, go there and stay.

"Watch out," says my ship's cook, "if you're coming here with your windy ideas just as a pretext for snitching an apple, because the next thing I'll do is smash your skull with a billet! Uphill, downhill—all nonsense! If you want to sit around and let your imaginations run wild, then do it. I have no time for it. I still have to prepare something for tomorrow. Come, Pedro, give me a hand. Don't pretend you're tired, *muchacho*."

As I leave, I hear the start of the next round. "But it just happens to be called the Green Sea of Darkness, and no one has ever seen it before."

García goes along to the bow in the rocking gait that's the safest way to move forward here on deck, and I fumble along behind him. I've no idea what he wants there. "It's on account of that Señor Sánchez," the cook growls, and waits until I'm up to his level to flick me a sidelong look. "He has a special permit from the admiral. Has kind of a sensitive gut, my lord *veedor real,* our royal comptroller. So he just happens to be unable to tolerate any pork. He's probably not the only one on board. Just the only one with privileges."

"What do you mean?" I ask uneasily, while my heart begins to thump in my chest.

"What else? We're killing a chicken."

In the turmoil of the past few days, I haven't taken in that there are actually chickens on this ship. They're kept in a portable coop, closely crowded together, and are obviously so intimidated that they haven't uttered a sound yet. But maybe they were seasick? In any case, they don't look as if they would lay any eggs. They're probably intended for García's stewpot only.

"The brown one there in the corner," says the Basque, opening the door of the coop. "That one already looks about ready to kick the bucket. Now, go."

I realize with mounting dismay that I'm supposed to grab the animal with my own hands—a warm, twitching, struggling creature, a creature that is slated to die.

The cook wrongly interprets my hesitation and says, "Just grab it by the wings, then it can't get away. Be quick," and he draws the machete out of his belt.

"No," I say tonelessly.

"Hey, boy," García says warningly. "Don't try any tricks here. Do you want a box on the ears?" Then he looks at me. I feel my lips trembling and press them together desperately. "Hm," he growls. "Haven't you ever done this before?"

I shake my head dumbly. I seem to be in a kind of paralysis.

"I'm afraid I can't let you off," says García with a sigh. "Maybe if we were alone. But whatever you do here, half the ship is looking on. That would bring many more questions than perhaps are good when you're involved. So: Either you grab the chicken or you whack it." He holds out the machete to me. "Come," he says energetically, "don't play the pretty boy."

I can't grab it. Something that's afraid. Something that might escape. My fingers would open by themselves and let it go—for what? For a howling pursuit over the entire ship, from the top down—who was the bumpkin that let it go? That grummet? Well, he'll get his thrashing. . . .

I hold out my hand for the machete.

García reaches into the coop, and with a sure grasp in the swirl of flying feathers and the wildly despairing cackling, he grabs the animal destined to die and lays its neck on an anchor winch.

I take the executioner's axe in both hands, just as Judith struck off the head of Holofernes when he was besieging Jerusalem. Suddenly a wild feeling of hatred surges through me. Yes, kill, retaliate, pay back what people have done to me and mine! It's only a chicken. A chicken for the great Converso Sánchez. I squint my eyes tightly and strike. The blood sprays in a high arc. García lets the body fall, and the headless torso runs in a bloody shower across the deck, amid the laughter of the men.

"There, you see," I hear the cook saying. "It went fine. I'll give you an extra serving of soup for that, too."

"Not necessary," I say. Then I faint.

Chapter Six

Blood, everywhere blood. On the steps of our house, in the streets of the *judería*. Even the water troughs at the wells in the Jewish quarter are colored red. It's unclean blood, they say, it deserves to flow. There should be only Christian blood in Castile from now on. Therefore the Castilian, for his salvation, has opened an artery and lets the heretic blood stream out. . . . Blood on the walls of the houses, where it has sprayed or spilled. But sometimes it's also used to make a picture with, the way a painter uses color. A cross of triumph, perhaps, over a man with a hat and tallith, a prayer shawl, who stands at the stake on a pile of wood . . . a six-pointed star that has been daubed over with a Christian cross.

No, no! No further, Pedro! Then I feel the heat at my feet, I smell the smell. . . .

"God's death, leave the boy alone, or you'll have me to deal with!"

I open my eyes, and at the same moment a flood of water is poured over my feet. García is standing astride me, the bucket in his hand. Between my toes there are stuck two frayed rope ends, whose ends are black. Obviously they've burned—the stake at my feet.

"Where we come from they call that an Andalusian auto-da-fé. Little troublemaker. Figured that'd make him get up on his feet again!" I make out the voice of my mate Alonso, and several laughs. Not so García. He's hopping mad. "Andalusian roguery is what I call a thing like that! But why should we expect anything else from you southern bastards? Singeing the feet of your own shipmate! Bah! Shame!"

"Now, don't get excited," someone else says. "It was just a little joke. And I'd like to know exactly what our being from the south has to do with it."

"You can find out exactly what below deck after the next watch, if you have the guts."

"Sure! Below deck and after the next watch! All the Basque cowards talk like that when they want to sound big. Here's where the music plays, and this is how the guitar looks!" And to my horror, he pulls his cutlass half out of its sheath.

García stands there, legs wide apart, looks him up and down, and then says calmly, "Oh, look, a knifer! We northerners are especially fond of those. One of the kind that would rather not rely on his fists. Well, no wonder. They're all just jellyfish. And besides, I have a knife, too." He holds up his kitchen knife, still red with the chicken's blood, and then he spits at the other man, and it lands exactly in front of his naked feet.

A loud murmur rises from the Andalusian faction.

"Whoreson! Basque fishhead! Just come a little closer!"

Just don't! Just don't let them begin to fight or use me as an excuse, either! Unthinkable what that could lead to for me! I sit up quickly and say, "Let it be, *muchachos*. Don't get all excited. It really was only a joke, García. Thanks for standing up for me. Don't do anything foolish, all right?"

On wobbly knees I stand up and then remove the charred rope pieces from between my toes. Really a mean trick to play on anyone. I try to laugh. "It's not so bad."

They keep standing there facing each other, measuring one another like fighting cocks in the ring. A few Basques have also joined García now. Then to my relief the Andalusian turns away and says, "It's not worth it for the half-pint. Another time, maybe."

The fellows grumble, but they're probably glad the situation hasn't come to a head. They at least have enough understanding to realize what would happen to them if they went for each other's throats. Certainly they'd come before the mast and receive a lashing. So they'd rather leave it at threats, and then again they have me as a target.

"You had to fall on your back on me!" García scolds.

Alonso and his friends sneer. "What a softie! Such a little mother's boy! Can't kill a chicken! Tips right over! Can't look at blood!"

"Perhaps I've just seen too much blood," I say rashly, but luckily it doesn't occur to them to ask more.

García presses the bucket into my hand and says, "Well, if you don't want to see it, then scrub this mess off the deck."

And with that the incident is over. I breathe a sigh of relief. Once more, things have turned out all right.

While I'm swinging the bucket into the sea on a rope to pour out the reddened water and get fresh, I notice I'm being observed. It's the fourth of the "gentlemen passengers," that interpreter, Luis de Torres, the one I heard praying in Hebrew when he was seasick. Will he likely get some of the *veedor real*'s chicken soup? In any case, I don't like the way he's watching me at all. If only I could figure out how I should behave toward him. Sometimes I think it would be best simply to speak with him about it. But then I'm overwhelmed with doubts. It's much more likely he assumes that, shaken with seasickness and being the poor dumb devil he takes me for, I didn't catch on at all to what he was doing. So I grin at him as simple-mindedly as I can, but it's probably too much, because he starts back as if I've stuck a dagger in him.

Or is such a smile from a moses too much familiarity for a person of rank? But I'm the moses who works as a page for the admiral. . . .

Of course. He understands that I have more savvy than the ordinary grummet and that I serve in the *toldilla,* so he's afraid of me.

Well, good, or much more likely bad, but there's nothing to be done about it. I can only keep quiet around him. Perhaps then he'll realize that he has nothing to fear from me.

No, it can't be the class distinction. As I'm rinsing the deck I can see that he's not too fine to talk with one of the peons, and he even seems to be making overtures to Alonso.

Next I'm assigned to work with the others unstacking the supplies in the stores room and sorting them. This is important. The stores have to be moved so that they don't spoil and aren't eaten by rats and cockroaches. My ability to write makes me very useful to Diego for this. I stand there with a slate in my hand and make tallies according to the numbers Diego gives me. So many sacks of chickpeas and beans, so many barrels of pickled meat, so many jars of olives, dried fish fillets, and stomachs of cheese . . . sometimes the *despensero* takes a random sample to check the quality. Every once in a while there's a fraud perpetrated during the loading in port, with bribed sailors secretly exchanging the goods purchased for those of lesser quality.

My work is easy. Except for the stench and the heat here down below, I have no complaints. But I'm a thorn in the peons' eye. "Do-nothing! Coward!" one of them snarls at me as he drags a net full of *vizcocho* past me. They never miss a chance to jostle me when the stores-keeper is looking the other way. I have to stay very alert. But it doesn't do me any good. When Diego briefly sticks his head out a porthole to let the wind cool his sweaty forehead, one of the two helpers lets a small flour barrel drop on my naked foot with full force. I cry out.

"What's wrong, Pedro?" asks the *despensero*. I feel faint. "Nothing, *patrono*," I say through clenched teeth. "I hit myself. My stupidity."

I carefully lift the barrel, pull my foot out from under it, and move it. Nothing seems to be broken, luckily.

The fellow who did it spits into the bilge in the ship's belly. "You're lucky you didn't squeal to that Basque, lit-tle fellow," he whispers hoarsely. "Wouldn't do you any good, either. Know what we do to squealers?" Quick as a flash he grabs for a big cockroach as, startled, it darts this way and that, trying to hide in the dark. He presses the creature between his thumb and forefinger. It snaps horribly. Both peons laugh.

My watch ends with the evening prayer, the sung Salve Regina. The crew kneels on the deck, caps off, and bawls the song. It sounds awful. The admiral doesn't show himself during this exercise. He prefers to talk with God alone in his *toldilla*.

My foot is fat. I draw up a bucket of water and cool the swelling. I've become so used to the up and down of the sailing voyage now, it's like the rocking of a cradle to me. I'm leaning against the mast, daydreaming, and my eyes are just about to close when I hear the mate's voice. "Where's the grummet? Where is that damned Pedro? The admiral's waiting for him."

THE TABLE IS DECKED IN ITS BEST. There's fresh fish—earlier, while I was still busy in the stores, García cast out a troll line. And bread, real bread, instead of rock-solid hardtack. Olives, vinegar and oil for the cheese, a pitcher of wine, dried apricots, almonds and raisins for nibbling. All the dishes are firmly fastened to the table.

There are places set for the admiral and one guest, the tall Gutiérrez, Don Misterioso. Am I by any chance supposed to serve here? My mouth is watering with hunger. I haven't eaten anything for an eternity.

But I can't let that stop me. Maybe I'll learn important things here, things that are essential, even . . .

"Pedro," the admiral says, not unpleasantly, "how long must one call you? Were you asleep?"

I swallow. "Yes, Your Grace. I was asleep," I reply. Even if he's not looking directly at me, I know nothing escapes him, neither the tar-and-sweat odor wafting off me nor my limp.

He takes an apricot but doesn't eat it, only turns it between his fingers. "People sleep much more than is necessary. I intend to try to do without sleep on this journey, insofar as it's possible. You should do it, too. Now, pour some wine for the gentleman. And then get the writing materials from the cupboard. There may be something to record."

Carefully, so as not to spill with the rolling movements of the ship, I fill the glass of the tall man, who leans back to avoid my stench, and limp to the bound chest to get paper and ink and quill. Since the table is covered with food, I sit on the floor, legs crossed, and hold my writing materials on my knee. It's better, in any case. This way I don't have to look at the food.

"I don't think there's any reason to record anything here," this Gutiérrez says. His voice sounds whiny, with that arrogant nasal tone that's supposed to be the fashion at court and is attempted by every little provincial nobleman.

But sometimes his tone changes. It sounds shrill and hard and takes on a disconcerting sharpness—and then it reverts to the court tone again. It's like someone pulling his dagger out of the sheath and then shoving it back again.

His eyes also make me uneasy. Even when his mouth smiles, his eyes don't. They remain sharp and watchful the whole time, and when he thinks himself unobserved, they dart from one corner of the room to the other, as if he were looking for something.

"So, no recording!" he repeats, and this time it seems almost to be an order. "I have nothing more in mind than to present one question, *almirante*. One question does not need a record."

"You're right there, Don Pedro," Columbus agrees. "But first, please help yourself. Fresh fish. Real bread. Then ask."

He is impeccably courteous.

The guest obviously obeys the command to eat. I hear him going about it noisily. The admiral eats nothing. I look at his two hands. The one continually turns the apricot. The other hangs down idly. But it doesn't keep still. The fingers spread; it clenches into a fist, then opens again. I had a cat once. She used to extend and withdraw her claws in just the same way.

In the meantime, Don Misterioso has finished his meal, and now he twangs nasally, "My question regards the course the fleet is taking at the moment."

For a long moment the fingers are still. Then Columbus asks, "In what capacity do you wish to put this question to me?"

A laugh. It sounds incredibly arrogant. "But Don Cristóbal, you know very well that I am only a passenger. Admittedly, a paying passenger." There it is again, the daggerlike sharpness in the voice, the threat. "After all, it's an open secret that not everyone can go along on this ship. To put it bluntly, I had the good offices of His Majesty King Ferdinand. Now, that's not the point." The voice becomes oily again. "I've undertaken to sail with you, mindful of your promise to reach the Indies within a voyage limit of seven hundred fifty leagues, sailing always westward. And what must I observe? The caravels are on a south-southwesterly course."

There is silence for a moment. Columbus's fist is clenched so tightly now that his knuckles turn white. Then he says, sounding very restrained and courteous, "I admire your nautical knowledge, Don Pedro. Really astonishing for someone who is not a seaman."

Gutiérrez laughs loudly and scornfully. "You haven't only fools to deal with on this voyage," he says. "Some people pay attention."

"Most certainly. What fault do you find with the course?"

Now the other man's voice is even more like a knife blade. "Well, someday I would like to arrive at where you pretend to be sailing to."

"What fault do you find with the course?" Columbus repeats, and now there is also sharpness in his voice.

Gutiérrez retreats from the demand he's just made. "Please don't get excited, Don Cristóbal. It's utterly unnecessary. I have no fault to find with the course, *almirante*. No one would presume to find fault with your orders. You're the leader of the undertaking and have the confidence of Their Majesties."

"So?"

"I would merely like to understand it."

The admiral's hand, the moving hand, now makes another gesture. Demanding attention, two fingers are extended in my direction and moved back and forth. I understand. I'm being commanded to write. So, as soundlessly as possible, I dip the quill and move it across the paper, trying not to make any scratching sounds.

"Now, *señor*, we are in the process of heading for the Canary Islands."

"To what end?"

"With the end of having the caravels caulked and sealed once more before the great voyage, changing sails on the *Niña*, and taking on fresh water and provisions. Satisfied?"

"Not entirely yet, *almirante*. Not entirely yet."

"I'm listening."

"Isn't there the danger when you put into an intermediate port that some anxious characters will think again and desert?"

"I've taken that into consideration, Don Pedro."

"You've taken it into consideration?"

"Certainly. I can't use such undecided men on the voyage. I will replace them with others. Their Majesties' secret orders permit me to take on crew anywhere. Even criminals can sign on with me; an amnesty will be granted them."

"I'm aware of that, *almirante*."

"You're aware of that? Astonishing. Very few people are aware of it."

"Well, as one who gets around at court, one hears this and that."

My quill rushes over the paper. If this Gutiérrez weren't so busy making himself look clever, he would have to hear the rustling and scratching. Meanwhile the admiral's hand has balled into a fist and stays that way. His voice, however, is unfailingly under control and soft.

"Was that all? If so, I would beg to conclude this conversation, which does me much honor. My duties call me."

"Certainly, Don Cristóbal. Is it true that Your Grace carries with you a letter from Their Majesties to the Great Khan of China?"

"About that I have no account to give you, Don Pedro."

"Who's talking about an account? It is only that this letter leads one to conclude that Their Majesties are expecting to penetrate rich and fabled lands to carry on trade and make political contacts."

Silence.

"But how does that equate with the cargo of glass beads, mirrors, and toys, such as one gives to the natives in Berber lands as the price for gold and slaves?"

The admiral has stood up. "Don Pedro, I regret to have to end this conversation. Definitively end it." His voice betrays nothing.

Gutiérrez has also stood up. "It was an honor and a pleasure for me to have partaken of Your Grace's hospitality and to receive a hearing for my questions." He bows, goes past me without taking any notice of me or my activity, and leaves the *toldilla*.

He is loathsome, self-important, menacing. Nonetheless, I can't help finding his questions thought-provoking.

"BRING YOUR WRITING THINGS to the table, Pedro," the admiral says, "and read me what you've written." He shoves aside the remains of Gutiérrez's meal with a sweep of his arm to make a place for me, not noticing that he's tilted the anchored dishes and scattered food from the bowls over the table. A lake of vinegar and oil forms directly under my nose and spreads to the beautiful fresh white bread, which soaks it up—but at least there are no spots on the paper.

I've taken pains to get the conversation down as exactly as possible and stumble falteringly through my notes. He says nothing when I finish.

"I couldn't be more exact, sitting down there and working as quietly as possible," I say boldly. "Is Your Grace dissatisfied?"

"No, no, it will do," he replies. I look up at him. His

sea-colored eyes are dark with anger, and splotches of red color his face.

"That snooper! That rotten, crawling spy! *Serpente maledetto!*" he bursts out, keeping his voice low. "He can find his own way back from Gomera when we get to the Canaries! I'll sail off without him, *sì, è vero!*"

I keep very still.

"I *have* the letter to the Great Khan. And I sail wherever I want to, in whatever time and wherever it pleases me! Open the strongbox, Pedro!"

I follow his order. The compartment is unlocked. From the pile of papers and charts he removes a magnificent parchment, furnished with seals and written in the most beautiful court handwriting, which he puts into my tarry, ink-stained fingers. "Read it out!" he commands, and I wonder as I read why this is taking place now. After all, he can hardly intend to prove to *me* that he possesses authority.

"From the mouths of our many subjects and others who have come to us—" I begin, and he interrupts me. "Louder." I read on, and then again he orders me to read louder, at the place where it says, "We have ordered that our worthy captain Cristóbal Colón be despatched... we beg you to give credit to his account—"

I understand that he thinks he is being listened to, either by Señor Gutiérrez himself or by some hireling.

"So," he says when I've finished, taking the document

from my hand and locking it away again, "maybe that will satisfy them. Now, let's amplify your notes."

Do I see what I think I see? Is there something like a grin on his face? No, I'm not mistaken: Columbus is looking gleefully at the strongbox holding the documents. And I have a sudden sneaking suspicion. Is this facial expression only because of the lesson he intended to teach Gutiérrez, or is there something more behind it? I don't have time to think about my feeling, because now he's beginning to dictate to me. He has retained every turn of the conversation in his memory, and although I can't understand why he thinks it's so important, I admire his precision.

Right under my nose lies the marvelous piece of fresh bread sopped in vinegar and oil and a heap of raisins and almonds, and I'm literally trembling with hunger.

I'm just about to lose control and simply grab that soft white bread, stuff it into my mouth, chew, and swallow.... My quill makes an involuntary excursion straight across the paper. There's a long streak across my report. I can't hold my hand still. An expression of annoyance escapes him.

"Begging Your Grace's pardon," I say bravely. "I haven't eaten a proper meal for days."

"You were seasick," he says. "But you haven't been since yesterday evening. Today there was nourishing food, so far as I remember. Beets and pickled meat. You didn't eat?"

95

"I had *mal de mer* again," I say.

He looks at me. "Stop your work for a minute and take some of the bread."

"Thank you, Your Grace," I murmur, and I take pains, despite my murderous hunger, not to stuff and gobble but to eat in a mannerly fashion. He watches me and says not a word. Then he goes to the door of the *toldilla*, looks around outside, and closes it, despite the sticky heat in the room.

In a soft voice he says, "When did you have yourself baptized, Pedro?"

Chapter Seven

"I come from a family of orthodox Christians," I hear myself reciting mechanically. I would say that even when someone snatched me out of a deep sleep. It's the sentence for survival. But in the same breath I gasp out, "How—"

Not one word further! Don't admit it! Never admit it until you've been saved and can thank the Lord at the top of your voice and with head held high! I've impressed that on myself. But how shall I do that facing those eyes?

"It wasn't hard for me to recognize," he answers. The beads of the rosary are now circling through his fingers again. "I knew from the moment you addressed me at the embarkation. Your greeting was 'The Lord be praised' instead of 'Jesus Christ be praised.' My suspicion turned to certainty when I had you write. You're used to writing from right to left and put your quill at the top right for a moment. The matter of the pork has only confirmed my suspicion. You're a Converso—indeed, of the newest variety. I have still more of them on the ship. You're very skillful. But be careful. You know how the Spanish Christians feel about the Marranos."

I'm silent. I'm even more skillful than he thinks, for I am no Converso and no young man, and he hasn't noticed it.

He seems to read my thoughts. "Perhaps you're also concealing something else. I'll not attempt to learn your secret, never fear," he says, and he lowers his voice still more. "But remember: Besides you and me, there is a crew of thirty-eight on board. That means that thirty-eight pairs of ears are eavesdropping on you and thirty-eight pairs of eyes are spying on you. A ship full of enemies. All are looking to push the one who might stumble. Even the most miserable peon. And all on board are thinking of gold and power. That's why they are under way. I can't chide them for that, for I'm also under way for gold and power. But the Lord shows me the way."

He looks past me.

"Yesterday I gave the order to release you from watch. I've marked very well that it didn't do any good. I'm not blind. I see your hands and the tar on your shirt. I see also that your foot is injured. But I cannot and will not intervene. I can probably protect you from the officers and the officials, but not from the seamen. I myself have been on ships since I could walk, Pedro. I was even less than a grummet. It happens as it must. And perhaps it's also ordained by God, from high to low, from strong to weak. It is order. And there must be order on board, otherwise the ship is lost.

"Go now. I have things to do. See that they let you sleep. Tomorrow you have to help me with the notes and the log, and I don't like it when you make spots and ink lines on the paper. It should be easily read."

OUTSIDE, THE NIGHT RECEIVES ME, and I stagger along the deck as helplessly as though I'd just come on board this minute and haven't learned how to walk with a seaman's gait.

I'm beside myself with dismay—and at the same time I feel liberated.

Dismayed, confused by the strange words of this man, this ambiguous Genoese, who takes back what he says in the same breath and supports what he condemns, who raises me up and at the same time leaves me to stand alone. I must think about what he's said. Later. For now, it's such a relief to give up the loneliness of my secret, at least to a degree—and it's *he* who has relieved me.

All at once I think I couldn't have held out one day,

one hour longer, going around with this lie, without one single soul who knows anything about me. I desperately feel like crying.

Pull yourself together, Esther! I order myself. He warned you himself. Even for you to speak to yourself in your thoughts with your girl's name is dangerous and forbidden. You must not let go. Letting go means losing. You have your story, Pedro, the grummet. You're from an orthodox Christian family. Your parents apprenticed you to a merchant, so you can read and write. Your parents died in an epidemic. You ran away from the apprenticeship to fight against the Moors, the accursed infidels, but the war there was already over, *señores,* Their Catholic Majesties had routed the Muslim dogs and chased them over the sea to Africa. . . .

Desperate, I crouch in the darkness, adrift in the up and down of wind and waves, drifting toward the unknown on the rocking timbers, and I pray to heaven.

God of my fathers, God of righteousness, I pray, give me strength. Do not let me lose myself. It's as if I were tied and bound, but only so can I save myself. If one of the ropes of this bundle is loosened, the whole thing will fall apart immediately, like a tangle coming free. Then I'd be lost. Pity me, God of my fathers, give me strength.

I feel my eyes overflowing with the tears I've forbidden myself to cry. Oh, it's really good to cry in the dark. Only a little bit. A few drops of salt water, soon past.

Orders and calls ring out from somewhere in the dark.

I don't care. It's not my watch. There is no me at the moment. I allow myself the duration of half a night on this wind-tossed ship, under the snapping sails, to let the tears flow. And to imagine for myself how sweet it would be to tell him.

Don Cristóbal, my name is Esther Marchadi. I am the daughter of Rabbi Judah Marchadi of Córdoba, the wise, the lucky. He was blessed by the Lord and beloved by his people. There was a single drop of bitterness in the cup of his life: The Lord had given him no sons. But he had a daughter, and on that daughter he bestowed all that a son would otherwise have received. The daughter was allowed to study the writings of the wise with him and read the Talmud with him, and since the famed rabbi was not only a wise man but also a cosmopolitan friend of the sciences, she learned the Latin language so that she could read the books of those of other faiths and understand their ways of thinking.

When Esther was ten years old, the Lord blessed her mother's body, and the joy was great. All prayed for a son for the rabbi. But the ways of the Lord are unfathomable. The mother bore a dead boy and also died soon afterward. Now Esther was all alone with her father. She learned with greater zeal than before, which helped her over the pain and comforted her father. Sometimes he said that no son could have given him as much joy as she did.

Then Grand Inquisitor Torquemada began his work.

It was in March of the year 1491—the year 5251

according to our reckoning—when he found the case he'd been looking for: a converted fabric dealer named Benito García. Drunks had allegedly found a desecrated host among his goods. Under torture people confess to anything, and García confessed that the Jews slaughter Christian children and spit on the picture of the crucified Christ during the celebration of the Sabbath. The Inquisition needed no more to proceed against my people. But the war against the Moors was still not won. Their Majesties could not dissipate their strength.

Granada fell in January of this year. The walls were breached. Now Their Majesties could turn against the Jews. They want a purely Christian land.

My memory feels its way here like a small child who fears falling into a pit. If it dares too far, it will plunge into the darkness, and then horror will overcome me and I will be lost.

I have forbidden this child memory to go further.

Hesitantly it feels its way along the edge.

The day when they stoned Marta, my Christian *dueña,* because she wouldn't leave me and kept on working for the accursed Jews.

The day when my father cited the writings of the preacher Solomon: "Blessed are the dead who have already died. And three times blessed, those who have never been born." That was shortly before they knocked on our door and—

Stop! Stop, no further! Not one step further, or you

will fall. Go around the pit of horror, the way my feet did then, carrying me away from all those places I had to fear. I was already wearing these boy's clothes. And I went around all the small market towns so as not to smell the odor of burning human flesh and hear the cry of the crowd: Burn, heretic, burn!

When I got to my relatives in Segovia and they heard from me what I want to forget and must forget, they stared at me as if I were Jonah, who escaped the whale. They aren't particularly courageous people, those Marchadis in Segovia, and the same things I'd experienced were taking place before their very eyes and ears daily. So far they'd been spared. They said to me, "You have courage, and the Lord is with you, Esther. Otherwise you'd never have made it here. You'll be the right one to do what we have turned over and over in our thoughts but have not been able to do. For we will not get away from here."

It was true that the *judería*, the Jewish quarter, was already under the control of the Santa Hermandad. But one could very well get away if one only dared.

But they said further, "The Jews of Segovia are ready to pay for their lives and their stay in Spain, as they have always done. Go, Esther, and take what we have collected among us, along with this letter to the great Don Isaak Abrabanel, the representative of our people. He enjoys favor at court and has lent the king gold for his excursions against the Moors. He'll find it hard to close his ears to our pleas. We'll pay. Go to Abrabanel. He will help us."

They wrapped a sash around my thin body—I still have it in my bundle—and in it they stowed the money they'd collected and the letter to Abrabanel. And so I set out with their blessings. No, I wasn't afraid. Too much lay behind me. I succeeded in fulfilling my commission. But it was already too late. Don Isaak told me he had promised the king unimaginable sums if he would only invalidate the banishment edict, but Grand Inquisitor Torquemada was stronger. The Church had triumphed.

"May the holy ones of Israel escort you, daughter," Abrabanel said to me. "You have courage and strength. If you can save no one else, save your own life. Keep the money your relatives have given you, go to Palos, and try to get on one of the ships that my friend and cousin, Luis de Santángel, the king's finance minister, is outfitting to find the lands of hope. Go to the fleet secretary. He is bribable. Perhaps you'll manage to escape."

I have escaped, Don Cristóbal. That is my story. Or anyway, the part of the story that I would entrust to you, if I would entrust it to anyone at all.

What I certainly would not tell you, *señor,* is that Nature has done something in me that is almost a miracle and for which I thank God every day.

Shortly before this horror-filled year 5252 began, I went from child to woman and must, as is the custom with us, undertake the monthly purification in the bath.

But then, after everything happened and I crept into the trousers of a little vagabond and his dirty shirt and ran away for my life—then it went away again. Once again I am as I was as a little child. To be sure, every four weeks I feel a pulling in my belly and wait in fear for it to come again. But nothing happens, the Lord be praised. Hunger and fear have probably done their work. At least as far as that's concerned, I can't betray myself. I don't bleed. And who would blame me for taking that as a sign from the Most High? I will survive—survive as one who has not become a Conversa.

AT SOME POINT García has whistled me to him. "God knows I've got other things to do besides serving the chow to His Honor the royal comptroller if I have to cook him something special," he growls, "and Diego's busy elsewhere, too. Do you trust yourself to balance this pot here up to the afterdeck without spilling any? It's that damned chicken. And in the future, don't stir up such excitement around you, boy, is that clear? It makes for bad blood."

"I'll try," I reply, leaving open whether I'm answering the first part of his speech or the second. Meanwhile I'm wondering why he's sending me and not going himself— he doesn't appear to be so busy. Does he perhaps shy away from dealing with people of rank, or maybe he's just thought up the errand in order to give me a pointer at the same time?

The clay pot is so hot that I have to wrap my shirt-sleeves around it to carry it. It is covered with a *vizcocho*, on which rest the spoon and a salt dish. Carefully, with wavering steps, I transport my burden to the poop. I find the gentleman aft on a kind of sailcloth stool, with a board serving as an improvised writing desk. He is angrily trying to look at some papers that flutter in the wind. The lamp is smoking. When he sees me, he claps his leather correspondence folder shut and says angrily, "A voyage like this is a foretaste of hell. Are you bringing my dinner?"

"At your service, Your Grace," I reply, placing the pot on his desk beside the writing materials. Almost at once he begins to carp, "What, no white bread? No pepper? No napkin?"

I have nothing to say to that. He lifts the pot's cover and sniffs mistrustfully at the food. Tsk, I think, I can't promise that it's prepared kosher. It's only a matter of a sensitive stomach, after all. Don Rodrigo Sánchez is a beefy man with the black stubble of a fast-growing beard on his round cheeks and a heavy chin. It's definitely important to him to eat well. "Go to our quarters and tell my page to bring me a napkin. And here, take this with you, too. Carry it carefully. It's important correspondence."

"Yes, Your Grace," I reply. He gets busy with his meal, but before I can leave he looks up once more and asks, his mouth full of chicken, "Are you the boy who does writing for Don Cristóbal?"

"At your service."

"Aha," he says, regarding me thoughtfully. The food smells tantalizing. "So you're that one. Didn't you come with a letter to Don Escobedo?"

"Your Grace knows that," I say, bowing deeply. I don't like the attention from this powerful man. I don't like attention from anyone, except from one in particular.

"The admiral had a visit from Señor Gutiérrez," Sánchez continues. "Do you happen to know what the subject of their conversation was?" I shake my head. This talk is making me very uneasy. What does he want of me? I don't have to wonder long.

"You can earn yourself a few coins if you keep me informed about such conversations. If you can write, you're certainly a clever boy. You can observe something. It's all for the benefit of the admiral, boy. You'd be doing nothing wrong. Well, how about it?"

"I'm never there when the admiral talks with other gentlemen or captains," I lie. "I don't know anything, *señor veedor real.*"

"Aha," he says once more. He frowns. "As you will. Now, don't stand around here. You can think it over, after all."

He sinks his teeth into a chicken thigh, and I take to my heels.

Later I see Luis de Torres, that interpreter I caught praying in Hebrew, walk up to him and talk with him, and I catch him looking sideways over at me as he does so. But other things push it out of my mind. I forget that very high-and-mighty Converso as quickly as possible. I have enough other problems. And as for letting myself be turned into a spy, may a just God save me!

I set to work on the ship again, hoping that I'll be called to the *toldilla* once more, to my admiral. I catch myself thinking of him as *my* admiral, and it quite confuses me.

Have nothing to do with dreams, nothing to do with feelings, Pedro, I tell myself very seriously. Your job is just to remain alive. You may not let yourself go under any circumstances, and especially not as long as you are on this ship. But it's undeniable that some things on this ship make me very unhappy and others make me rejoice. Yes, I rejoice in the work for my admiral, who challenges me, sharpens my thinking, and quickens my senses. I rejoice in the new, confusing discoveries that I gain with him, and I await with excitement the moment when I can look deep into those eyes and make certain they really and truly have the color of the ocean.

This is merely a tiny piece of life. What can be wrong in that? I'll be kept within bounds. Of that I am very certain.

Chapter Eight

I work hard all the next day, scouring the bilge with vinegar water to prevent rot, moving little sacks of ballast here and there, smoking the stores to drive out the vermin. Sometimes I'm standing up to the ankles in foul, brackish water—the sailors think we'll have to pump soon—and I nearly faint from the stink, but at least I'm by myself and don't have to watch out for the tricks of the others. Rats, spiders, and cockroaches I'm not afraid of. Things like that can no longer make me tremble. When I was still Esther, a well-brought-up young girl, I screamed with disgust like any other girl when my cat caught a mouse or a rat and laid it at my feet. In the meantime I've grown another skin, whether I want to or not. What more could a rat do to me?

We continue to have heavy seas and are sailing with

the wind. The caravels dance before us like two large white butterflies flying over the surface of the ocean. Often they must shorten sail in order not to outrun the clumsy *Santa María* by too much, and the admiral is clearly vexed at our plump tub and keeps giving impatient orders for nautical tricks that will make better use of our sail power. The men get no rest at all, hanging in the shrouds and yards, burning their hands on the damp ropes, cursing and laughing. But the mood isn't bad. I overhear the owner, Juan de la Cosa, murmuring to the pilot, "This damned Genoese is sailing like the devil!"

Finally, at the break of dawn, Columbus orders me to him. Again he works with compass and ruler on the chart, enters the course and speed by dead reckoning, and explains his estimates to me. Then I help him construct his real and false logbooks. It puzzles me, how quietly and matter-of-factly he goes about it. He lies with utter conviction, as it were. But after all, I'm doing it, too. We are equals in lying. The difference is that I know the reasons for my lies. They're vital to my survival. His reasons are unknown to me—or at least it seems to me that what he's told me isn't sound. Pedro Gutiérrez's questions occur to me again. I, too, would be glad to have them answered.

Then we go to the aftercastle, where it's comfortably fresh at this hour, after the heat of the day. The steady breeze sweeps through my linen shirt and cools my salt-chapped skin. It blows the admiral's hair around his forehead. The bow wave hisses past on both sides of the ship like a foam-crowned wall. Over us the stars are very large and close enough to grab.

Columbus has taken the quadrant out with him and is now looking at a star that I think is the pole star.

"Why is Your Grace doing that?" I ask softly. "I remember you taught me that this instrument is valueless on a moving sea and is only useful when the ground underfoot is steady."

He stands with legs astride, the apparatus in his hand, a large silhouette against the sky, and says, "You're right about that. I do it for the ship folk, so they'll admire my knowledge." I can barely keep from laughing out loud. But he means it quite seriously.

"Can you determine the course according to the position of the stars?" I ask.

He lets himself down on the rail and sits there without holding on—a maneuver that would cause me to fall overboard immediately. "You can do that on the Mediterranean," he explains, "not here. This is another ocean, with other laws."

"But how can you navigate, then?"

"I've already explained that to you," he replies, a little impatiently. His fingers drum a rhythm on the tarred bulwark below the rail. "I have the compass. I estimate the speed we're making. I thought you understood that. I know the weather."

"How can you know the weather? The Lord God alone provides the winds."

"May He be praised forever," he says, crossing himself. "It's as you say, Pedro. But He provides them according to laws that He Himself has created. We can learn to know these laws through experience. I've traveled by ship within the limits of the known world. I've been in the lands of perpetual ice and in the blazing south. There's a system to the weather. In a harbor in England named Bristol, the difference in water level between ebb and flow is about twenty ells. I've seen it with my own eyes. It's the power of the moon over water that does that. Warmth and life-giving winds come from the west. You use them when you travel toward Guinea. You can rely on them. Again, others drive you constantly toward the setting sun. I'm counting on those on this voyage. One can measure and calculate."

"I admire Your Grace," I say softly.

"It's good to talk with such a clever young person," he replies. "I wish someone with your powers of perception had been in Salamanca when I presented my thesis to the doctors of theology."

How have I demonstrated my cleverness to him? I've only listened, after all. "Were the gentlemen not amenable to your arguments?" I ask, and I sense the rage rising in him. He stands up, takes a few steps, gets hold of himself again. "I think," he says in a controlled voice, "they considered my arguments a subject for joking. But

God has granted me the victory. Come with me to my cabin. You shall read something to me from a book."

"Gladly, Your Grace. As you command."

He goes ahead of me, mentioning as we go the number of knots the ship is making and the number of leagues we will have sailed by this night.

"You are a great seaman," I say reverently.

He replies, "I am the greatest seaman of this age." He says it so casually, as if he were informing me which of the harbor taverns in Lagos has the best paella.

IMAGO MUNDI—PICTURE OF THE WORLD—is the name of the book I am supposed to read to him, and it comes from the pen of a cardinal from Paris. It's written in Latin, and I already know it. Rabbi Judah once gave it to his daughter to read—with a smile, for it's quite a simple text compared with scientific works such as those of Ibn Esra of Arabia. Really, the Parisian theologian only put together old texts on geography and on the view of the world that came from the authors of antiquity.

But when I open it and page through it, I see something that fills me with excitement: The book teems with marginal observations in his handwriting, the wonderfully clear, easily legible, small handwriting of the mapmaker who is accustomed to drawing a contour in one sweep, never lifting the quill from the paper.

The pilot calls him outside, and I use the opportunity to page greedily through the book.

For a person like me, a person who has grown up with books and has gotten to know the world through writing, the handwriting of a person is something magical. It's a part of his own self and belongs to him, like his skin and his hair. Anyhow, I sense in the marginal jottings, even without knowing their content, the spirit of the Genoese in a way that makes me shiver.

In some places he's drawn a tiny little pointing finger to mark the importance of the text. Not an arrow or an underline, a finger! I bite my lip. It looks so playful, with the humor that he doesn't have at all in dealing with his men—and I think of *his* fingers, those long, slender, constantly moving fingers. . . . Most of his annotations are in Spanish. They are astonishingly simple. So simple that at first glance you don't even grasp how significant they are. As unpretentious as stones, as the foundations on which you erect a building. *Every country has its west and its east,* it says here, and in another place, *The ocean is studded with lands.*

In the bars of Palos and Moguer they scoff that Don Fantástico wants to voyage to the West in order to find the East. Yes, that's so. A Latin note here: *Totum mare navigabile.* All seas are navigable.

I lift my head and look outside, into the oceanic night, through which our keel plows on a journey that hasn't even really begun yet. *Totum mare navigabile.*

He's walked up behind me, as quietly as a ghost. "Light new wax candles," he says, "but make sure you

114

don't let any drip on the book. It's important to me. And then read me the Ptolemy selection. Read it and translate it."

Most of his annotations are in the Ptolemy selection in *Imago Mundi*.

"Why does Your Grace wish to hear Ptolemy?" I ask. "I saw that you've already been very much concerned with this author."

"Yes," he answers simply, "but there's much I haven't understood. Or I'm not sure that I've understood. My Latin is very inadequate, you know. It will make it easier to think if you translate."

WHAT AN ABYSS OF SLEEP I sank into, and how sweetly and peacefully I awaken! No evil dreams have visited me. I lie soft and comfortable, and on the threshold between sleeping and waking I think for a moment that I'm the girl Esther in the house of Rabbi Judah and I'm lying in my bed. My body has the memory of a gentle touch during sleep, as if someone has stroked me with a downy feather, as if the wind has blown through my room.

When I open my eyes, I see white curtains around me. The curtains of my bed in my father's house were of brownish brocade.

I sit up. I've slept in the admiral's bed.

In panic I'm wide awake immediately. The first thing I do is feel down my body. But, thanks be to the Eternal, I'm still in my clothes stiff with tar and salt water. Are these knots just the way they were yesterday? I can't re-member. Anyway, I'm belted and fastened up to the neckline.

What happened? I was reading from *Imago Mundi* and translating. Somehow sleep must have overpowered me. Probably my head sank onto the book and in the middle of a word I fell silent, perhaps even tipped over one of the candles. Unimaginable! What a situation! And Colum-bus? Did he call me? Did he perhaps shake my shoulder and realize that my sleep was as deep as an infant's, that nothing more could get through my exhaustion?

And then, instead of calling someone from the crew and having me carried out, he lifted me up and put me in his own bed, covered me, closed the curtains, and went out to look at the stars again. . . .

A seething warmth spreads through me. I see myself in the arms of the admiral, my head on his shoulder—all at once it seems to me I'm aware of his scent. Certainly it's lurking here in the covers and pillows, a strong, good, powerful scent, not comparable with the stench of us unwashed crew members. I'm dizzy. And what if he'd gotten the idea to open a few lacings of Pedro's shirt, so the boy would be more comfortable? Once more I look at the knots. I have no idea. . . . Did he see my body? Did he touch me? The images and feelings that plague me are so strong that they even keep my terror in bounds—I must stifle them utterly and completely! Be on your guard, Pedro!

But I am sixteen, after all. At this age you sometimes need a little sleep. The admiral's advice that it's best to avoid sleep altogether—well, even he probably can't follow it entirely.

I am sixteen. Until now that was a completely factual statement, and if it had anything to do with feelings at all, then it was the bitter wonder that as a Jew I'd succeeded in becoming sixteen in the year 5252 without having been slaughtered before now. All at once it has an entirely different flavor. It has something of challenge and hope. I am sixteen. . . .

Pedro, just be careful.

Slowly I push the bed curtains aside a little and look into the room.

The *toldilla* is empty and full of sunshine. I don't know what watch is up, but in any case it's morning. I must think how to get out of here somehow without anyone noticing. What would happen if they did doesn't bear thinking about.

I'm just about to pull back the curtains when I hear steps. Two men are coming into the cabin, and in terror I throw myself right back on the bed, flat on my stomach, holding my breath. Who is the admiral bringing with him? Does he assume I'm already gone?

But then I hear that it's not the admiral at all. A voice that I can't place says, "Don't worry, he's busy up at the bow now, setting the course with smoke signals. It will take some time."

And the other one answers, "Good, good. I'm very much indebted to you." I know the second voice well. It's the nasal, whining tone of Don Misterioso, Gutiérrez, whose conversation with the admiral was of so much interest to the *veedor real*, Señor Sánchez. "I was quite startled," he continues. "It's said we're going further on a western course. No one has spoken about the islands. And now we're obviously sailing very close to Portuguese waters. Is there treason afoot? I've never trusted him—please excuse me—even if you are close to him. And His Majesty King Ferdinand doesn't either. So, you think he has a secret chart?"

"I'm very sure of it," answers the first voice. "Of course, I've never seen it, but my cousin has told me of it. The chart was in her house, and it must be here on board. Here in these chests."

I hear him trying to open the locked chest, while I'm feverishly trying to think whose cousin he might be. Did not García, or was it Diego, say that the provost, Arana, is related to a mistress of the admiral? "Even if you are close to him"—certainly, it must be the *alguacil,* the provost.

Meanwhile the discussion goes on. It's carried on in low voices and quite fast.

"And you think it's not Toscanelli's map, on which he showed Their Majesties our sea voyage?"

"If we were sailing according to Toscanelli's chart,

we'd be sailing straight toward the sunset, yes? But we're not doing that."

"*Señor alguacil,* I smell outrageous betrayal. He's hand in glove with these Jews. The *veedor real* is working with him. All these heretics have only one goal: to undermine our holy faith and deceive Their Catholic Majesties. That must be prevented!" His voice almost breaks.

I hear the lock of the strongbox clatter. "If anywhere, the paper is in this box," Arana says. "Before we left he had extra iron bands made for it and ordered a second key. He's a very mistrustful man."

"Where does he keep the key?" Gutiérrez asks, and Arana says, "If I know him, he has it on his body or in the pocket of his coat. Perhaps he keeps it under his pillow?"

I press even flatter on the bed, holding my breath. My palms are damp.

"Under his pillow? No, no!" Gutiérrez laughs softly. "He doesn't sleep, as everyone knows. . . . Señor de Arana, it is very important. We can still stop him in the Canaries. In return for your loyalty to the Crown, I know the right people to speak to. There will assuredly be a place at court for you."

"I do it very unwillingly, Don Pedro," replies the provost hypocritically. "After all, he lived with my cousin, and I am bound to him."

"Señor de Arana! This course! South-southwest!"

"Your Grace, it could also be that the reason for this

course is of an entirely different nature. It lives on Gomera and has black hair and green eyes, and sometimes state secrets turn out merely to be love affairs."

"It doesn't matter. And when we get back . . ."

"Yes, when, Don Pedro. When. But that also probably depends on this chart. Whether we arrive. Where we arrive. Whether we get back."

"How do we get hold of this paper?"

"I've already thought of something. But let's go now. Someone could see us, after all. Perhaps that boy who's always going in and out of here can . . ."

And with that they're outside, and I sit up, bathed in sweat and with trembling hands, and try to understand what I've heard and make sense of it.

This Arana, the admiral's protégé, intends betrayal, selling his patron to the lords of the court. Secrets, another chart that Columbus keeps for himself, fear of a conspiracy with the Jews—Sánchez, Santángel, the other course—my head is swirling. And what's that about a love affair and black hair and green eyes?

What was that at the end? "That boy who's always going in and out of here"? Now am I supposed to spy not only for Sánchez but also for the officials of the Crown?

I sit there quietly for a moment in that bed, trying to pull myself together. Then I draw the curtains back, slip into the room, and peer around outside. The coast seems to be clear.

Bent, I hasten out the door of the *toldilla* and down

from the afterdeck to the hatch, where I encounter no one but the interpreter, who gives me one of his strange looks. But he's the last thing I can think about now.

My foot still hurts, and I have to favor it as I walk.

García is busy at his hearth. "Hey," he asks, "where've you been rambling? Your friends were asking for you."

"My friends?"

"Well, that other grummet, Alonso, the Andalusian. He acted quite important. When do you have watch?"

I have no idea when I have watch, because I don't know how late it is. "Right now," I say, just in case. "But Alonso isn't my friend."

"I wondered, too," growls the ship's cook.

I've been avoiding that nasty Alonso however I can, hiding behind Diego and García and the duties to the admiral. But the *Santa María* is too small for us to run away from each other for long.

Chapter Nine

I find Alonso amidships behind a couple of rope coils and a bilge pump, throwing dice with two of the peons, and one of them is the fellow who dropped the keg on my foot in the stores.

But even before I get to him, I stumble and bang my head hard against a cross rib. A rope lying in front of me on the deck was pulled tight just at the moment I walked over it.

My head is throbbing so hard, I'm holding my temples. The three dice players are looking over at me, grinning.

"Hey, boy," says Alonso. "You're in such a big hurry!" And they all bellow with laughter at the joke. Suppressing the pain, I say, "I heard you were looking for me. What's up?"

"I looked for you a long time," replies the grummet. "Were you taking a nap in the bilge or something? Well, no hard feelings. Come on, have a drink with us."

I'm handed a *bojito,* and so I won't seem like a spoilsport first thing, I hold it up and take a gulp, but I immediately spit it out again in a high arc. It's salt water, if not something very much worse. It makes me gag till my eyes water. The three are watching me intently. They'd probably like it best if I now were to throw myself on them, as then they could beat me and still truthfully maintain that I began it. But I pull myself together, toss the *bojito* back at them—Alonso immediately tips the contents overboard—and say with forced calm, "Enough fun and games, all right? What's going on?"

"The boy's pretty curt!" remarks one of the peons threateningly.

Alonso says, "What's going on is that while you were dreaming away, it was your watch, *mozo.* And that makes trouble."

Mozo! Friend! What's that supposed to mean? I'm not part of your gang, I think, while terror courses through my limbs. Hastily I try to figure back. I have no idea if it's true. But I don't intend to let myself be browbeaten.

"You just made that up!" I reply. "Besides, it was ordered that I be free from duty on the ship, and Señor Chachu knows that."

"Oh, you don't say!" sneers Alonso. "The admiral's lapdog! How are your delicate little hands and your poor little foot where something fell on you? I think you should be in bed!"

I notice that more of the men are becoming interested in this quarrel. Two of the dark-bearded fellows who always keep to themselves are hanging in the shrouds, listening, and still another hulk of a peon has come and planted himself there, his arms crossed. Alonso continues, "Free from duty! There's no such thing, boy. There's already enough idlers on board here, that Basque just happens to be right about that. Overseers, provosts, doctors, interpreters—all standing around and eating the real seamen's bread. It won't do you any harm at all to pitch in and do your work."

I have no wish to back down, especially not now.

"I *do* do my work—in the *toldilla*," I say.

Now they're all laughing.

"Nando here, he saw what you do there! Draw scribbles on paper! Is that what you call work? That's child's play."

"Child's play if you can do it," I reply. "Can you? Then do it."

He stands up and comes over to me. "Don't go too far, little friend," he murmurs. "Many a man has gone overboard during a long sea voyage. The rail isn't so high, after all. And otherwise—there's all kinds of little things that'll make you wish you'd stayed home with Mama." He stares into my eyes.

I've already had a few tastes of the kind of thing he

means, just now and before this, from a crushed foot to the "Andalusian auto-da-fé." I don't have any desire to get myself harassed. Absolutely none.

"So what do you want?" I ask. "What's this about the missed watch?"

He snorts. "No one was at the sandglass," he says accusingly. "My friends Concho and Nando, both honorable gentlemen from Palos, can bear witness, and so can Juan there. The pilot, Don Pero, came and yelled, 'Which of the grummets is supposed to turn the glass?' and Señor Chachu said, 'That Pedro, but he's sitting on the admiral's lap!' and then I stepped forward, because you don't leave your friends in the lurch, and yelled, '*Señor pilato mayor,* I'll take over the watch for my friend, the little fellow can't help it!' So that's how it was."

The others have stopped throwing their dice, intently listening for the outcome. I'm silent, thinking. I feel very uneasy.

What he's saying could be true, but it could just as well be a lie. Even as hostile as this crew may be toward the Genoese, they still maintain respect, and when the pilot learned that I was ordered to the admiral, he would have assigned someone else to the watch. And that one then didn't show up—that's how it would have happened.

"Good, *mozo,*" I say. "May God reward you. I'm grateful to you for it.

"I can of course take over a watch for you. Except

there's one thing I don't understand. You just said before that I was dreaming away during my watch. And then that I was with the admiral. So which is it, now?"

He's got himself muddled, and that makes him even angrier. "Better not risk yourself a fat lip!" he threatens. "Your mates can help you if you're nice. Or they can let you get into trouble. That happens very fast when we all stick together. A rope gets unfastened or a water barrel tips over or a sandglass breaks, and we all swear up and down that it was the grummet Pedro. Señor de Arana has the say in cases like that, so it won't do you any good to be the pet in the *toldilla*. You'll be stripped, tied to the mast, and have the pleasure of making the acquaintance of the nine-tailed cat. It's much too quiet on this voyage, y'might say. Not enough happening."

That's a threat that really frightens me. Of course they can manage that. And it would be the end of me. I bite my lips. "What do you want, Alonso?" I ask. "You know I have nothing. You've pawed through my bundle yourself."

He says nothing to that. So it's probably true. He's silent, considering. Then he says, "We don't need any paltry maravedis from you. Have you forgotten what Captain Pinzón promised us? We'll all be wading in gold over there in the Indies. We have something else in mind. But I'd rather talk to you about it alone."

Where can a person be alone here?

But my fellow ship's boy has obviously thought about that.

"Come on," he says. "We'll go sit in the craphouse together."

I get hot all over. That's all I need! "But I don't have to!" I say, and then luckily something better occurs to me, and I add, "What'll the others think if two boys go in there together? That there's something going on between us or something?"

Alonso screws up his eyes. "Hm," he murmurs. "You've probably had some experience with that, eh, lapdog? But for once you're right. Good, we'll go up in the shrouds." Agile as a cat, he scrambles high up in the rigging ahead of me, never looking back to see if I'm following. For good or ill, I have to go after him. Courage, Pedro, I tell myself. This is the lesser evil. You'll probably be able to hold on properly and put one foot in front of the other. He certainly won't climb all the way up. My mouth is very dry with excitement. So, up after him.

"Come on, you lily liver!" Alonso calls down to me from the yard where he's seated himself. "Good God, what a fuss you make. Now, come on, hurry up."

Finally I'm sitting there, holding on desperately and looking out over the churning sea and the deck of the *Santa María*. I realize that it isn't as bad as I thought at all.

And now Alonso comes out with it.

"That gibberish that you read out of the big book—is that the language the admiral curses in?"

It's true that people all over this ship are listening. Columbus is right.

"No," I answer. "That's Latin. Like what the priests in church talk in."

"Ha!" says my freckled friend. "Then he wasn't lying to me."

"Who? Who wasn't lying to you?"

"That's none of your business. My affair, understand? But I need someone who knows Latin, and my friends do, too."

"How come? You want to understand what you're praying?" slips out of me, and it's immediately clear to me that I've gone too far, for Alonso says softly and threateningly, "Another remark like that and you'll fly right off of here onto the deck."

"Fine," I concede, but I can't help holding on a little tighter. "So now, out with it. What's this all about?"

"It's about the island we're going to."

"Many islands."

"Poppycock. The admiral intends to put in at Gomera. Everybody knows that. The *gobernadora* is a witch. She's supposed to have hexed the admiral."

"Oh? Really?" I ask, and I have to swallow hard because my mouth is even drier. Alonso nods and continues, "On the island there's a church. And there's a story about it. Many heathen used to live on the island. But the *gobernadora* had most of them killed. . . ."

My thoughts are somewhere else. The ruler who is a witch, and Arana's talk of black hair and green eyes—do they mean the same woman?

"What? How?" I ask. Alonso is already a bit further in his tale and demands indignantly, "Aren't you listening to me?" I nod, and he says, "I'd advise you to. So. And then they all go through the side door of the church." (Obviously I've lost a piece of the story.) "But she has them all killed, on consecrated ground. A bloodbath. And the last was their king, who was a sorcerer." (I have no idea what he's talking about, and so I nod eagerly.) "But the king had an amulet that made him invulnerable and invisible. And as he lay dying—"

Now this is too wild for me. "How could they have killed him if he had an amulet like that?" I ask.

Alonso snorts angrily. "He didn't have it around his neck, it was in his hand," he lectures me, as if it's clear as daylight. "When he lay dying, he had himself baptized by a young priest. He entrusted the magic thing to the priest and made him swear to bury it in the church in a place where his enemies couldn't find it. The priest did it, and in three places in the church he wrote in Latin how a person could find the amulet. Then he got sick and died. Only he never told anyone else what the thing is and where the inscriptions are."

129

He falls silent, and I'm dizzy, not only from my seat in the airy heights but from this utter madness that he's told me. What does he actually want from me? "Yes? And?" I ask.

He looks at me as if I were the ultimate idiot. "Don't you understand anything at all? The one who told me knows where the inscriptions are. And you know Latin."

Finally it dawns on me. Alonso wants to be invisible and invulnerable. . . . Whoever could have dished up this nonsense to him? "Can I ask something?" I inquire carefully. I take his silence for agreement and go ahead. "This priest or monk—why didn't he use the amulet himself?"

"Because it's heathen magic," whispers Alonso, quickly making the sign of the cross, which I prefer not to do because I can't hold on firmly enough with only one hand.

"And what do I have to do with it? Why doesn't your sly friend go himself and get the thing—for himself or for you?"

Alonso shakes his head. "Because *he* doesn't know that language," he replies. "But he heard you gibbering. You know it."

"So, he's here on the ship?"

Alonso is silent. "He knows the way," he says then. "You can read it." Why doesn't this mysterious unknown just deal with me directly? Why should the grummet Alonso, of all people, get the magic thing? Did he ever ask himself this? He wants to talk me into being a kind of church robber, if I understand it right. Whatever do they have in mind? Are they really that stupid or are they just pretending to be? But Gomera is far away, and now I'm on the *Santa María,* and if anything is unwise, it would be to get into any more conflicts with these fellows than I already have. They'll harass me to death.

"And me?" I ask. "What do I get out of it?"

"When I have the thing, I'll protect you!" promises the future invisible and invulnerable Alonso grandly. A dreadful prospect.

"We're not there yet," I say. "*I* want something now. Make sure that no one plagues me anymore. I want my peace on board. Tell the Andalusians to leave me alone. Tell your friends the peons that I'm all right. That I'm your friend. Then I'll do it."

He looks at me, considering. "All right," he replies finally. "Done. And now climb down. We still have to seal it."

What does he mean by that? Well, I get to find out right away. He jumps down beside me on the deck and calls one of the peons over.

"I've just made a bargain with him, and now he has to swear. Help me."

Now I learn how it works when you swear something with a Christian like Alonso. I'm forced to my knees. My left hand is held fast so I can't renounce secretly and the right hand held high. "Now swear by the life of your mother and by the Virgin and all the saints that you'll do what we've agreed."

I can easily undertake the oath. I can't perjure myself at all, for my mother is dead, and for me the Virgin and all the saints are just like the colored figures in the fairy tales of the *Thousand and One Nights*.

The men around me are laughing.

"And you? Do you also swear?" I ask. He spits. "My word is good," he answers, turning away.

Sometimes I think this is not a ship but a lunatic asylum.

Chapter Ten

The "conversation" with Alonso keeps going around in my head as I wet the deck and scrub it with a brush of elder. And I wonder once again what the whole thing means. But we're not in Gomera yet, and the truce I've bought lets me breathe easier. For the moment, anyway, there won't be any tricks from the direction of Alonso and his uncouth friends. By the way, I asked Chachu. No, I didn't miss a watch. That was a monstrous lie. I play the dialogue over in my mind again to get a clearer idea of the person who spun such a tall story and what he might have had in mind. It seems like a trap. But is it set for me, or am I only the bait? And who's making use of this fool Alonso?

That's one thing. The others are the two lofty gentlemen I involuntarily overheard in the *toldilla* who want to get at some kind of secret of the admiral's and who obviously also think that "the boy," that is, I, must play a role in it.

I have a very uneasy feeling. Here we are, only three days under way, and I've made every effort not to attract attention. And already I'm entangled in several things like a fly in a spider's web.

This *Santa María* is not exactly a stronghold of peace, but I didn't expect that, either. It's enough that I'm alive and on it.

Is it really enough? Confused, I regard my face in the mirror of the bucket of seawater. In the swashing surface I see my exhausted face, deep shadows under the too-large eyes, forehead and cheeks burned by the sun, and that long nose, covered with scaling, peeling skin—how ugly I am! I compress my lips. As if that were important, Pedro. Angrily I pour the water across the deck with a big swing.

You're becoming cocky, Pedro. You had a chance to get enough sleep for once, your stomach is no longer growling. You can visit the necessary at night in peace, if Alonso isn't right behind you—but perhaps he won't do that anymore now that I've given in to him like soft butter. Furthermore, I've even learned to empty my bladder in a heavy sea . . . and they all stink here anyway.

Grummet Pedro, what do you want? Better keep hold of yourself. You've escaped with great difficulty and have to fight to fall asleep at night without dreams haunting you from the grave of your past. And after a few days on this floating tub you're worrying about how much uglier you've gotten! You should truly be joyful if no one looks at you. Joyful that nothing indicates who or what you really are.

But I am not joyful. I confess to being wholly and completely discontent at the thought that the gray eyes of that man in the *toldilla* perceive me only as a plain-looking boy with a halfway intelligent head and facility in reading and writing.

Yes, Esther Marchadi, and so have you gone completely mad? This is the admiral of the ocean seas, a man of forty years. You are a thing of sixteen. And the very first place he is sailing is to a witch with green eyes and black hair—

Oh, right. I must find an opportunity to report to the admiral on the visit of the two gentlemen to his cabin, and as soon as possible. On the other hand, perhaps there's hardly any danger that the two can so quickly find a chance—My thoughts are abruptly cut short by an announcement from the lookout, a call that I don't understand. As the usual hectic activity begins, the admiral appears on the poop, shading his eyes against the sun with his hand, and looks in the direction the signalman seems to be indicating. I let my bucket and brush stand and rush to the rail with the others. To the windward, the *Pinta,* the beautiful, gull-like caravel, is sending up excited smoke signals whose meaning I can't read. She's turned and dances in the wind with rattling tackle and fluttering sails. At the rapid speed we're making, she falls quickly behind.

In the minutes that follow I look on with breathless admiration as the crew of this ship carries out its officers' commands.

Columbus gives his quiet orders, never shouting, and they are quickly and precisely executed by de la Cosa, by the pilot, and by the mate, Chachu. Reef sails. Heave to. Command *Niña* to also heave to. Signal *Pinta* that the admiral is coming on board. Lower the ship's boat—it all is a matter of two or three Paternosters. Suddenly this *Santa María*, on which everyone is pitted against everyone else, this spider's web of intrigue, is a united, functioning organism. Only the passengers are in the way, running excitedly back and forth and keeping the crew from their work.

Heave to: what a sensation! All at once it's quiet. No wind whistling through the rigging any longer, no bow wave hissing along the sides any longer. The ship rolls and lurches with an extraordinary movement and gives out complaining noises, moaning and groaning. My sense of balance threatens to vanish. I become dizzy and have to hold fast to a rope, though nothing is moving at all.

The rope ladders are lowered, and the admiral is hastening to follow the oarsmen and Chachu, who will probably steer, down into the boat when his glance falls on me. Naturally I'm standing gaping at the rail, like all those who have nothing to do with the operation. He says nothing. He only points his finger at me. And I, tightly clutching the sides of the swaying rope ladder, climb down into this boat that is pitching on the ocean dunes like a horse with a rider on his back for the first time. I close my eyes.

"ALMIRANTE A BORDO!"

Captain Pinzón, his mouth twisted even more awry in the dark stubble of beard, his eyes snapping with anger, receives us. The *Pinta* has rudder damage. The rough seas have lifted the heavy iron rudder off its hinges. We learn that two of the pintles, iron bolts that hold it in position, are broken off. The third is holding, but the *Pinta* is virtually unmaneuverable.

Repairs are being undertaken even as Pinzón invites us into his cabin. Four seamen, among them the cooper and the ship's carpenter, are being let down from the outside and are fixing the damage. Perhaps it's not so bad. But Don Martín pours his heart out to the admiral. To him, it's sabotage, no question about it, and of course it's by Cristóbal Quintero, the ship's owner, who's been an obstructionist from the beginning because he wasn't able to captain his own ship. And furthermore, because he's afraid his tub could be lost on the voyage, he signed on as a simple seaman, with the single goal of keeping the *Pinta* from sailing beyond the Canaries.

"He knows all the men!" says Martín Pinzón. "So it doesn't take much for an agreement. And maybe he even tampered with the rudder back in Palos. . . ."

"Have you proof?" asks the admiral. "I'll make the guilty one answer for it and have the ship's provost—"

"Proof?" interrupts Pinzón, snorting with rage. "The rudder's in two pieces! That's the proof!"

We're in the captain's cabin, and the gentlemen are drinking wine, which I must serve them—I realize it's the admiral's trick for keeping me with him. Naturally I figure that he'll again want me to write up a record of the conversation afterward, so I'm keeping my eyes and ears open.

"That's not proof, Don Martín," the admiral says. "That's like asserting that the mill is round because the mule walks in a circle. I can't do anything on the basis of that. Have you questioned Quintero?"

"He's lying! Obviously he's lying! The hypocrite even asked to have a hand in the repair work—supposedly because it has to do with his ship! Yes, damn it!" Pinzón's fist cracks on the table surface, and the admiral crosses himself, which I quickly do after him. "He has nothing else to do except think up the next act of sabotage!"

"I can't follow your argument," says Columbus coolly. "It's laudable that you've tried so quickly and energetically to repair the damage. But I can't imagine any man who owns a ship maliciously destroying it himself. So long as you have no real proof, I ask that you maintain peace on board. The Lord has other plans for us than to allow the men on the *Pinta* to knock heads over small squabbles. Do not forget, Captain: These ships are in God's hands." He stands up, his gray eyes fixed on Pinzón. "I hope your people have luck with the repair. But if it can't be patched up, you should by all means call in at the harbor on Gran Canaria. There are excellent shipbuilders there who know what to do. Should the *Pinta* be irreparable, I will see about getting another ship."

The knuckles of Martín Pinzón's balled fists turn white. Controlling himself with difficulty, he says, "Does that mean a new crew as well?"

"Certainly not, Captain," Columbus replies courteously. "I need your experience. But think, you would then be free of shipowner Quintero."

Before we are rowed back to the *Santa María*, the admiral surveys the work on the rudder and nods in approval. "That is solid and reliable."

Cristóbal Quintero and his brother Juan, both wearing red caps, approach us. Their faces are dejected. "The captain doesn't wish us well, Admiral," says Juan, the younger. "He accuses us behind our backs of treachery."

"Has he reason to, *señores*?"

"His only reason is that part of the crew is sworn to *us* and not to him," replies Cristóbal. He's a thin, gray-haired man with a hooked nose, the type who tends to be hotheaded.

"I won't listen to that sort of thing," says the admiral, turning away. "On any ship, everyone is subject to the command of the captain. And you, *señor*, have thus to see that your people behave accordingly. Avoid disagreements. As for the rest of it, I am convinced of your honesty."

TOWARD EVENING the *Pinta* signals the completion of the repair, and the ships again begin making way as fast as they can. The admiral calls me into the *toldilla*.

"Your Grace sees me still ashamed," I say as I enter with head bowed, "because of yesterday evening. I fell asleep over the reading." I can't keep my voice from trembling. When I was out there on the *Pinta* under the eyes of many men, it was different. Here in the closeness of the cabin and alone with him, I feel apprehensive and excited at the same time, uncertain and churned up. He laid me in his bed—

"That's forgotten, Pedro," he says casually. "Come here now and help me."

Only now do I notice what a remarkable activity he is engaged in. He's holding a piece of silver lace in his fingers and a long, gleaming needle and is busying himself with his velvet cape. Obviously the trimming tore off as he moved vigorously about.

"Nobody on board has a hand for this. The men can only mend sails. Can you try it, Pedro, with your writer's fingers?" He throws the things into my lap, and they all promptly fall to the floor because I spread my legs—if a person has worn a long dress all her life, that's normal. "Hey, not so clumsy!" he says angrily. "Not a promising beginning. Nevertheless, try it."

With uncertain fingers I try to get the thread through the eye, and although he isn't looking over at me, I have the feeling he's observing me. "Tell me," he asks abruptly, "what you think of the damage on the *Pinta*."

"It's not my place to examine the words and deeds of Their Worships the captain and officers—"

"*Basta, basta,*" he interrupts me. "*Tutti gli annessi e connessi! Parla!*—I mean, don't mince words."

"I understood that very well, Your Grace," I say. I still haven't got the thread through the eye, and he takes the things out of my hands and in a single, calm motion moves the needle onto the thread—not the other way around, as I have learned it—and says, "That's how you do it. All the rest is woman's stuff. I come from wool merchants and silk weavers." His tone resonates with a sound of "as you know," as if all the world must be interested in his antecedents. "Now then, the damage."

"I think," I say as I watch his fingers do the handwork as fast as a weaver's shuttle, "that the damage on the *Pinta* is entirely ordinary, caused by the heavy seas, which are probably too much for such caravels, and that Señor Quintero had just as little to do with it as anyone else."

He nods, bites off the thread, and lays the mantle to one side. "You see, that's how it's done," he says. I'm very uncomfortable with this interlude. Why is he instructing me how to sew on trimming? "And Pinzón?" he asks tersely. "What do you think of Pinzón?"

Why really is he examining me here? My opinion of Pinzón will hardly influence his, after all. I can't contain myself any longer and ask, "Why does Your Grace want to know that of me? I'm only the ship's boy here."

It seems to me a shadow of amusement flits over his face. "Right," he replies. "So don't get above yourself. In spite of everything, you are at the moment the only one here who has an independent mind. Not too independent, I hope. That's rarely good. Think simply that it amuses me to listen to you and that I'm using you like a good dog, to which one also talks sometimes." He looks at me searchingly. I compress my lips. How tender!

"But now your answer!" he commands.

"The captain can't stand anyone but himself," I say carefully.

"The captain is eaten up with ambition and lust for gold! I think him capable of any treachery!"

His face flushes. He balls his fists.

"But Your Grace himself signed him and his brother on in Palos, or so I've heard."

"I'd have found no crew without him," he says softly. "A few murderers and cutthroats who saw a chance to escape punishment through the amnesty, but no seamen. I wouldn't have gotten past the islands we're heading for now with them. Moreover, in Palos they were thumbing their noses at me and the royal edict, saying yes, yes, but doing nothing. Without the Pinzóns I didn't even have a ship, Pedro. They are first-class seamen. But they are pirates, plain and simple. They lured the crews with the gold that we're going to find, and the men trusted them. Robbers find trust in robbers. Martín Pinzón wants to be the first one to arrive in the land beyond the water, and he wants not just treasure but also fame."

"How could that be possible, since everyone knows that Your Grace alone conceived the bold plan and convinced Their Majesties?"

"Pedro, the falsehood of the world is enormous, and envy has brought down many an upright man. There are many who are envious of me."

I nod, considering whether this is the appropriate moment to tell of the two men in his cabin earlier today, when I lay in his bed and held my breath. And since he obviously really does divine what one is going to say (or what I am going to say!), he turns around to me so fast that his chair almost tips over. "Is there something you're keeping quiet, Pedro?"

I feel my face grow hot. "There was no chance today, Don Cristóbal," I reply, and he snaps, "It's not your place, Pedro, to decide for yourself when you report something to me and when you keep it back!"

His anger strikes me like a blow in the face. I stammer, "G-good master, God be my witness that I didn't intend—"

"To toy with the trust I place in you?" he finishes my sentence. I nod vigorously. I feel as if I were enveloped in flames.

"So, report!" he commands, without softening the sharpness of his rebuke.

"I woke up when they came into the *toldilla*," I say haltingly. "I would almost certainly have run right into them. But I found myself still there—" I point to the bed with the closed curtains, and he nods. "So I heard what they said."

"Who?" The question is like a rapier cut.

"Don Gutiérrez. And Señor de Arana, of whom it is said that he . . . is related . . . to Your Grace, and therefore I half thought also that he might perhaps be entitled—"

"He is a cousin of Doña Beatriz, the mother of my son," he says casually, as if the whole ship must know by which of the women of Castile he has children. "And he is *not* entitled. Go on."

I report to him of the talk in front of the strongbox and try to recapitulate it as exactly as possible: the search for the keys, the promise of a reward. Also that the last words that I heard were about me and that I'm afraid they intend to get access through me to the thing they're seeking.

When I'm finished, Columbus is silent. He's turned his head away, and I can't see his face. Finally he says, "Thank you, Pedro. The coincidence and your youthful sleep have done us good service." The brusqueness is

144

gone from his voice. "It's always useful to know of treachery in time."

"I'm fumbling in the dark, Your Grace," I dare to say. "What kind of a chart is it about? And in whose service is Don Gutiérrez working?"

"As far as the second question is concerned, I'd like to know myself, Pedro. I don't really want to speak with you about the first, although your alertness and your interest please me. So: The secret, too, belongs to the nature of the voyage. All great captains had their charts, their records, their tricks, which were known only to them. In the shipping company offices in the city I come from, people call that *discrezione*." He considers for a moment and then translates into Spanish, *"Delicadeza,"* and I must smile at his taking such pains, for the word *discreción* exists in Castilian, but obviously it doesn't correspond to what he wants to express.

"But the key," he continues, and I lift my hands to stop him from going further. Not that! *That* I do not want to know! *"Almirante,* don't tell me things that are none of my business!"

The shadow of a smile hovers around his lips. "You're right," he says matter-of-factly. "And now leave me. I want to enter the experiences of the day alone in my personal logbook. You can resume your labors tomorrow. Go now."

I don't know if he's still angry with me or whether he mistrusts me as well. I search his features, but he isn't looking at me, and when I grab for his hand in order to kiss it, he withdraws it with an abrupt motion.

GARCÍA IS PUTTING OUT HIS FIRE when I come up to him. "Annoying," he grumbles, running his hand through his thick hair. "The *despensero* forgot to ask the admiral if he wants a warm meal tomorrow. Now I don't know when I should start a fire." He looks dubiously over at me. "You're in and out of the *toldilla*," he says. "Could you ask?"

"I don't know," I say hesitantly. "I can try."

I run up to the cabin on the aftercastle. My naked feet slap softly on the ship's deck. Usually he notices even this approach immediately. The door to the little room is open, and I stop on the threshold. But Christopher Columbus neither sees nor hears me. He is praying.

I've seen the Christians pray in their churches and know that they talk differently with God from us Jews. I've seen them crouching as penitents or with arms spread, as if they wanted to mount the cross of their Lord; I've seen them with folded hands and closed eyes, usually humble and tearful. But never yet have I seen anyone praying like the admiral. He's kneeling in the middle of the room, not like a penitent but with his body taut, erect, more perhaps like a vassal of the king about to receive the tap of knighthood. He has the cross of the rosary pressed against his chest with both hands. His head is raised, and I sense that his eyes are wide open. He's in a serious, urgent dialogue with Him. Reflections from the light of the candles dance restlessly over his white hair, and he speaks raptly the words of the Psalms of David: "In thee, Lord, do I take refuge; let me never be put to shame." And once more, demanding, almost angrily, "Let me never be put to shame!"

I withdraw as softly as I can. "I couldn't speak to Don Cristóbal," I tell García.

Chapter Eleven

*T*he next day the seas are even higher, the wind freshens, and the three ships are again making good speed. On the horizon the mountains and cloud-like belt of the islands rise out of the mist, and when I have nothing else to do, I stand forward, in the bow, staring across at the land, the first land I've laid eyes on after five days' sea voyage. *"Tierra a la vista!"*—land in sight! When will we hear this call from the crow's nest the next time, and what will we get to see then? The Indies?

But at the moment, we aren't arriving at either the Indies or the Canaries. The *Pinta* signals renewed damage. This time we don't go on board but have a report delivered from there. Shipowner Cristóbal Quintero, the "saboteur," comes across to the flagship himself, climbing up the rope ladder with the most subdued expression in the world. "That damned pirate gave me hell!" I hear him say to our pilot, and we find out that their rudder has really broken this time. And on top of it, the *Pinta* has a leak.

The admiral rages. A leak! What does a leak matter! Leaks are routine affairs! Why else are there coopers and caulkers on board? If Martín Pinzón is acting this way already, before anything has begun, so to speak, he really wonders if he has the right captain on the caravel!

He strides angrily back and forth, stops suddenly, and addresses Quintero gruffly. "Tell Don Martín that I do not intend to lie here and wait until he finds a solution! I will go on ahead with the *Santa María* and the *Niña* and hope to meet up with the damaged vessel at some point in the harbor at Las Palmas."

Quintero hems and haws. Does the admiral expect him to repeat this to his captain word for word?

"Why not?" asks Columbus, still loud, and Quintero says, "Because I'm afraid that then we'll be going at each other with knives, Don Cristóbal!"

"What kind of ship's discipline is that? Do your duty, Señor Quintero, and don't feed me horror stories like that. You're a seaman on board, so obey your captain. And beyond that, obey your admiral. Or shall I send the provost, Señor de Arana, over to the *Pinta* with you so he can make sure there's order?"

Quintero leaves the *Santa María* very downcast, and I find Columbus's behavior quite incomprehensible.

Yesterday he took Quintero's side. Today he's dressing him down. Besides, I'm not very happy to have the voyage continue so quickly. Because then the superstitious and dangerous business that I'm supposed to perform for Alonso comes close enough to touch, and so far I have no idea what I'm going to do. And as if the God of my fathers has seen my fear, the stiff breeze drops and finally the wind stops altogether. The tips of the islands disappear in the mist. Nothing more. The admiral has all the sails reefed. *Con botavara seca*—with drying spar—we ride on the swells.

IT'S HORRIBLY HOT. But on a ship, a calm doesn't mean you can sit with your hands folded. Immediately we're commanded to tar the hull, overhaul the pumps, repair the rigging, splice ropes, flood the deck with water and scour it. Really, it's easier when we're under way. Then it's only a matter of getting the essential things done, fast and well. In between times, the crew can rest. Now we are harassed by the owner, Juan de la Cosa, Pilot Niño, and Mate Chachu, all at once.

The gentlemen passengers keep getting in the way everywhere, hindering the crew as they work.

That interpreter always makes a wide arc around me. Sometimes I see him whispering with the fleet secretary, and it seems to me they're looking at me. But perhaps I'm imagining it.

Meanwhile, the admiral paces back and forth on the

aftercastle like an irritated lion. The delay is obviously a hard test of his patience. He also calls a council, consisting of the shipowner and pilot, fleet secretary, and royal officials, perhaps to get approval for what he's going to do when the calm ends and he sails on. I don't know. I'm not there. As fleet secretary, Señor Escobedo keeps the record. That's why he was brought, after all.

Incidentally, I'm not the only one who notices that the curly-headed *alguacil,* the general provost, Diego de Arana, is not invited to the meeting.

By evening not even the tiniest breeze has come up. At least the calm gives the crew the opportunity to jump overboard and cool off in the sea. However, many just let themselves down on the drag lines that are set out for catching fish: They can't swim. It sounds so absurd. The majority of Christian seamen consider the skill of swimming a work of the devil. They say that when a sailor gets into distress, it's best if the Lord takes him to Himself quickly, before he tortures himself swimming around for hours and then drowns. There is a certain logic to it.

I don't go into the water. I swim very well, but I'm afraid that people might see my modest figure outlined by the wet clothing—at least what I *don't* have would be noticeable—and so I declare, "Water has no deck, my grandfather, God bless him, always used to say. Besides, too much cleanliness isn't good for you."

They laugh. If they only knew how I long for a cooling, cleansing bath!

Toward evening the ship's doctor is called in to the admiral.

"Change of weather," says one of the men. "That's when old wounds hurt."

"What kind of wounds?"

They are sitting together, I among them, with legs crossed, the great sail between us, and it's growing dark. People fall into conversation. I'm feeling comfortable, since no one is bothering me. Alonso seems to be keeping his word.

"Don't you know? He was in a sea battle twenty years ago. By Cabo de São Vicente, up there in Portugal. He was on a Portuguese merchantman, in a convoy with five other ships. Heaven only knows what the moneybags had loaded. Anyhow, a freebooter made her way up to them, and it came to swordplay. The Portuguese lobbed fire, but the wind was strong and the ships were too close together. They all burned. Masses of dead! God have mercy on their souls."

The men cross themselves mechanically and, since they've already dropped their work, the *bojito* also circles around; this time it clearly contains more wine than water.

"What about our admiral?"

"He's supposed to have taken an arrow and jumped overboard just in time to swim to Lagos. Sometimes swimming is useful after all."

A dispute over the usefulness of being able to swim starts. It's all very peaceful.

But on this ship, no such state lasts for long. Someone in the crew says, "Look who's sneaking up! The long-nosed Marrano from Moguer!" In fact Maestro Bernal is approaching us sail menders, casually avoiding the outstretched leg of one sailor, as if he hasn't even noticed that the man is trying to trip him up, and he says in a friendly way, "The admiral needs a healing salve. I'm asking the grummet Pedro to come with me and take it to him."

I get up while the gentlemen of the crew express their contempt for the Marrano with belches, grunts, and whistles—however, they don't dare attack him with words, thanks to the discipline on this ship. And also, a man doesn't know whether he might not need this doctor sometime.

Bernal doesn't take any notice of it. Back in the corner roofed over with sailcloth where he lives after a fashion amid his chests of medicaments and his surgical instruments, he stirs up a mixture of various powders and water and olive oil and says, "Not only can the admiral use this to treat his wound, he can put it on any spot on his skin. It makes it supple, relaxes, and stimulates the spirits when one is exhausted, but if the humors are in turmoil, it may also calm them."

"So, a miracle cure," I say, joking, and he throws me an

oblique glance as he says with an amused smile, "In whatever belief you use it." A not entirely unambiguous remark, it seems to me.

I sniff at the little dish. "Honey," I guess. "Lavender, lemon. Is that supposed to help with old wounds?"

"The admiral's wound is not at all critical. Our commander needs a medicine to give balm to his soul," replies the doctor, and now he is smiling at me openly. "Take it to him. He's waiting."

I take the mixture, and when I turn to go, I hear him murmur, "Beware of Luis de Torres. He does not wish you well."

Luis de Torres is the interpreter.

"I can almost imagine that," I reply. "But what does he mean to do to me?"

"I've said nothing," Bernal whispers. "I know of nothing. I only know that this man is afraid. Most dogs bite in fear."

I am sunk in thought as I walk to the aftercastle.

"I've been waiting for you, Pedro," the admiral greets me. "Enter yesterday's course in the second logbook—with the usual changes, as you know. Afterward I'll tell you what you should note."

"I've brought the medicine for Your Grace," I say, but he waves it away. I'm to put down the little pot and start my work. It's still light enough to be able to manage without candles. Furthermore, the small room so traps the heat that the additional flame from the light would melt us right away. The admiral drinks water from a *bojito* wrapped in damp cloths to keep it cool, and he gives me some of it. I drink it greedily—the wine I was drinking while we were mending the sail has created a pressure in my head. I must think clearly.

Under the admiral's eyes I take up logbook number two and copy the course he's entered in his private diary by means of the ship's position, undervaluing the distance and making changes in the direction, as he himself has done in these last days. He observes me in silence, without praise or blame, and then dictates his remarks to me, pacing back and forth in the small room. Always only three steps.

Because of the heat he's taken off his doublet, and it's hanging over the chair on which I'm sitting. He's very close to me.

When I've finished my work, he bends over me and checks the entries and the drawing. "Soon you can even do it without me," he says, and I take that as praise.

"My desire is only and always to please Your Grace," I reply.

He sighs. "I wish all the members of this fleet were of the same mind." His restlessness seems to be transferred to me. "Is there anything else I can do to please you?" I ask. I don't know how I could, but in any case I'd really prefer to be up and out of here. It's simply too hot.

"Yes," he says. "This salve. Maestro Bernal's balm. Put it on the scar."

"Wh-what? I should . . . ," I stammer, pressing my fingernails into the palms of my hands. Careful, Pedro! Don't forget that you're Pedro! Why shouldn't I?

He appears not to have noticed my exclamation at all.

He loosens the laces of his shirt, pulls it down off his shoulders in one motion, so that it hangs around his hips, and presents his back to me. Never yet have I seen the unclothed torso of a man so close, not to mention touched it. My head is swimming. I look at the structure of his powerful muscles along the spinal column, the broad shoulders, and the base of his neck. The scar is a small, raised ribbon that runs under his left shoulder.

I notice that my fingers are trembling when they scoop out some salve and carefully apply it. His skin quivers. "Firmer," he says. "It doesn't hurt."

My fingertips slide along the scar as if they were walking on a ledge, and they circle. I remember my nurse and try to do what she did when she stroked away a tummyache for me. He exhales deeply. "You do it very well," he says softly.

I gulp. What's wrong with me? I'm confused, I'm trembling. I have an uncontrollable desire to touch him further. So far I haven't even succeeded in kissing his hand. . . . "Maestro Bernal said this balm is not only intended for the wound. Would Your Grace allow me to rub more on you?" I ask, forcing a firm ring to my voice, and I'm intoxicated by my own boldness. My headache has vanished.

"Go ahead," he replies, letting himself down astride the chair on which I was just sitting, laying his arms on the back and his head on them. "If you think you're a master of that sort of skill?"

"It remains to be seen," I say, and I dip out some of the cream, but only enough to make my work-torn fingers smooth. And now it's as if I were obeying a power that comes not from my own short life, a power that is older than I am, that proceeds from my very depths. It's as if I were in a daze. I place my hands firmly and gently on his neck muscles, and again he quivers when they begin to move downward over his shoulders with gentle pressure.

I feel the sweat running out of my hair and down my temples in fine drops. His skin, on the other hand, is dry as tinder. Hot and dry. It seems to me that there, where my fingers are gliding along, sparks are actually going to leap up.

Slowly I leave his shoulders and run my hands down along his spine, feeling the strength of his muscles, and try to work less with my fingertips than with my entire palm, to ease him and to pass on to him the power that I feel in my pores in this mysterious manner.

He sighs. "You have the hands of a healer," he says in a low voice. "You do me much good, Pedro."

My palms are hot, my fingers are throbbing. From his hips I move slowly and gently up again, make little circling movements along his vertebrae, as if I were stroking a cat, then turn my hands, palm up, and press my knuckles between his ribs.

"Where did you learn that?" he asks, and I reply, speaking just as softly as he does, "Nowhere, Your Grace. The hour inspires me."

Again he sighs, this time much more deeply, from his profoundest depths. "I was full of unease," he says. "Now all my powers are gathering in me. It upsets me when the ship makes no headway. But now I know that I can use this night."

"That's Maestro Bernal's balm," I murmur, and he, "No. That's you."

It's still light outside. A gentle breeze rises, making the piece of linen in front of the *toldilla*'s window move. Without lifting his head, he remarks, "We'll have wind tomorrow, but from the wrong direction. We'll have to tack."

Is he already sailing away again, away from this hour?

As carefully as if I'd built a house of cards, I remove my hands from his body.

"You end things before they're finished," he murmurs, and I, "Finishing them is Your Grace's business."

"Yes, you're right there."

He gets up from the chair and orders quietly, "Help me undress."

Our eyes meet. He has never looked at me like that before. It's as if two fencers are crossing foils. He sits on the bed, and while I kneel before him to remove his shoes and stockings, he loosens the waistband of his trousers. My hands drop.

He breathes heavily, bites his lip. Then with a gesture that is careful yet firm at the same time, he presses his hands against my shoulders and pushes me from him.

"The Lord will give me rest," he says hoarsely. "He will send me sleep. Leave me. I thank you."

With an abrupt motion he turns away and closes the bed curtains in front of me.

"I wish Your Grace a good night," I say in a choked voice.

I don't know how I get to the door. I feel as if my whole body were in flames.

I took great pains not to see it. But I did see it. Not only that the flesh of Christopher Columbus was aroused after my touching. But also that the admiral of the ocean seas is circumcised.

BRIT MILAH, THE CIRCUMCISION, the removal of a boy's foreskin eight days after birth, is the sign of the Old Testament. It is through this custom that the Jewish child enters into his Jewishness.

It's a celebration, and I have taken part in this celebration often enough. I know what I've just seen. And I know also what it means. It's the seal of the covenant, and it cannot be repudiated. Only death ends it. I am the daughter of a rabbi. I know all about it. Whatever belief the admiral professes now, before God and in the eyes of the Jews he is a child of the Jewish people, a Jew.

It is the blessing of the Lord, and it is the curse before the peoples of the world. No baptism removes it. You cannot disguise yourself, as I am doing. And any Converso who in his truest heart professes another belief must tremble that the Christian mob of a bathhouse will expose him—however perfectly he babbles his Paternosters and Ave Marias.

I'm sitting in the shadow of the sails, crouched down, arms around my knees, and making an effort to keep my teeth from chattering despite the warmth of the evening. In vain I try to master the uproar of my senses and the jumble of my thoughts.

My head is in a fog, and in my fingers, now clutching my thin legs, there is still the knowledge of the body that I've just touched.

Pedro, Pedro, be careful! You've learned to put one and one together. You've learned to think in order to survive and . . .

I heave a deep sigh and groan. Lord, illumine my mind! I pray, although I can probably forget that. The Lord certainly has more important things to do than to bother with the confused head of a rabbi's daughter who is crouching on the deck of the *Santa María* in a calm and has just made a perplexing discovery, entirely by accident, after she has touched the skin of a man and has seen his sex, and that although she is only sixteen.

Yes. But yes. All at once a different pattern appears. All at once things become clear, things that I have been puzzling over since I slipped onto the ship with the help of my maravedis and a letter from Don Abrabanel. All at once I understand why the most powerful man next to the king and the most powerful Converso, Luis de Santángel, was prepared to finance this voyage and at this time—why there is a translator for the Hebrew language on board this ship and why the king's confidant absolutely insists on getting into Columbus's strongbox.

No, we aren't sailing to the Indies—or are we?—but even *if* we're sailing to the Indies, we're looking for still something else there—aren't we? I'll ask the admiral about it tomorrow.

All that has been vague speculation until now, all that I've assumed happened behind the admiral's back, as it were, or with only his half agreement, or with some kind of bribery—it has become part of a plan. The pieces are coming together to form a picture.

I feel drunk. My fear and uncertainty have turned into a feeling of great happiness. Is this supposed to be salvation, my salvation and that of my people? Should I have felt it with my fingertips there where I touched the back of the man who now sleeps in the dark hut on the aftercastle?

I stand up and walk over to the rail. The breeze has dropped again. There is still the calm, still the mist over the water. But up there the clouds part silently, as if someone has drawn back a curtain, and a few stars shine down on me. I can't help it. I spread my arms out, hum the first notes of a song that Marta taught me in the old days in our garden, and sway my hips. I'd like to dance.

And then a blow hits me in the back. I lose my balance, stagger, stumble, and pitch over the rail into the sea.

Chapter Twelve

You go down quite deep when you fall overboard from a ship. It's a terrible shock if you haven't gone into the water voluntarily. But when I surface, coughing and gasping for air, I'm all ready to enjoy this swim that I've avoided and someone else has bestowed on me, the incredible refreshment that the water brings. But of course I've let it be known I can't swim. Whoever pushed me over the rail most certainly wasn't wanting to do me a good turn. He intended for me to die.

I turn on my back, let myself float, and peer upward. The *Santa María* lies dark and ponderous over me, like a mountain. It's absolutely still. Only the light sloshing of the waves and the creaking of the wooden rudder and the timbers can be heard. There's no one looking down on me from above, and yet I have the feeling that, some-where, eyes are observing me.

Really, it's very simple. Lookout and helm are manned, and at least six men on this ship have "grave-yard watch." So I need only call loudly enough. The *Santa María* isn't moving, so she isn't going to sail away from me. There's no danger.

And after I've sorted this out for myself, I consider whether it's wise to call. I've just declared to half the crew that I can't swim—now I'm floating in the water. So why did I lie? I can always still call.

I circle the ship with long swimming strokes, trying to be as quiet as possible. García's drag lines are out. Possibly he's hoping that something will still bite at night. I consider whether I can hang on to such a rope on the side of the *Santa María* and then climb it, the way the boys in Córdoba climb the palms. But in the first place I'm no boy, and in the second place the hull of the ship is wider up there than down here. I don't even have to try it.

It's a crazy idea! I'll never get up there! So then, call? Gradually I begin to be afraid. This sea is unpredictable. It's not gentle and easily mastered like the waters of a river or of a still bay behind the breakwater. For this rea-son, even the swimmers among the sailors didn't let go of the lines when they swam. I have to be careful about where the waves carry me and use all my strength and skill not to be driven away from the ship. And as refreshing as this involuntary swim was at first, I'm slowly growing cold in the dark water.

I'm on the lee side now, where the sea is quieter, so I'm not in danger of being dashed against the ship's hull. While I'm looking up, trying to find another way to get up onto the *Santa María* again on my own, I discover a rope on one of the scuppers. Maybe someone fastened a bucket to it and then forgot it—a thing Chachu would certainly not let go unpunished. But perhaps I can use it. Right over the scupper is a port that leads to the freight hold. I wait until the ship's side rolls deep into the water, grab for the rope, and actually manage to catch hold of the scupper with the other hand. With great difficulty I pull myself up, scraping my stomach and almost falling down again on the other side when the ship heels over. I cling desperately, pressing my back against the tarred bulwark, astride this great pipe. Over me, but not within reach, is the port. So it's actually all different. My measuring eye deceived me.

Bending my head way back, I look up at the ship and spy a sturdy hook just over the port.

Lovely, but for that I need the rope again. And now that's hanging just out of my reach.

I can still jump into the water again and call. While I pause to get my breath back and balance my weight on this scupper, my eye falls on the rope I used to belt my linen shirt like the others, at the very beginning of the voyage. Luckily, I haven't had to work in the shrouds yet, so I haven't needed it.

The effort to free the rope is like being on a swing you can't hold on to, or riding bareback. The soaking-wet rope is stiff and resistant, and it feels as though it takes half an eternity until I've loosened it. On the other hand, it's easy to make it into a big loop, and somehow anger and desperation give me the drive to make the loop actually land over the hook.

Gathering all my remaining strength, I pull up and heave myself through the port. Finally, panting, I let myself roll down inside the *Santa María*, always wary lest my unseen antagonist has been observing me malignantly and is just waiting to crack me over the head now that I'm inside. When I go to dry my wet hands on one of the piled-up sacks, I find that I can't get them dry. It takes a moment for me to understand that my palms are bleeding.

After resting a moment, I sneak above, putting my upper body through the hatch as carefully as a wild animal walking out of the forest into the open country.

All around me are sleeping men only. No one is lying in wait for me. Everything is wonderfully peaceful.

With some difficulty I find my bundle in the corner where I kicked it, go into the stores in an unobserved recess, and change my wet things for the dry shirt and the other, even shabbier pair of trousers. I take the damp things with the bloody smear from my hands up on deck and hang them to dry on the capstan, the way the other men who went swimming did. Let him who pushed me overboard see it. I'm alive. Let all see it.

Then I go and carefully wake Maestro Bernal, who's sleeping on a sack between his medicine chest and his sea chest. He's wide awake immediately. I show him my hands. After all, I want to perform my writing duties tomorrow. He says not a word but salves and bandages me. I now have shapeless paws, like a big, clumsy animal. But my fingers move.

Only when I lie down to sleep near the hatch, where for a wonder there's a place, do I break into sobs. I'm exhausted. I press the bandages against my lips and stifle every sound.

NATURALLY THEY TEASE ME next day about my bound hands and ask me if a stingray came on deck, but I just smile and say nothing and scan challengingly for a face that expresses astonishment or guilt or a pair of eyes that avoid mine. But there's nothing like that. I also say nothing about my wet, blood-smeared clothes, and they wonder whom I could have fought during the night.

No, no. Of course *he* says nothing. I didn't even expect him to. Here comes his grummet and page with hands wrapped in white linen with only the fingers showing, and he says nothing. But I think today I will get him to speak.

Despite his prediction, we're still becalmed. He reminds me of a dish that's simmering over a low flame. On the surface there's nothing to see, but just stick a finger in it and you'll see how much heat there is. But I'm not made of ice, either, even if someone tried to cool me off in quite a radical way last night.

"What does Your Grace wish me to do?" I ask as I clumsily arrange the writing things with my bandaged paws, then prepare the two logbooks, the instruments for setting down the course, the correct and the false, and a pile of parchment pages.

A quick glance strikes me from his ocean eyes. Then he turns away. Did I see red in his face? For a moment there's silence in the room. Then he asks, "Why do you take out all those things—Pedro? You see as well as I do that we're making no headway today."

I look at him. He's back to normal.

"I thought you would perhaps want to make a few secret corrections again, Don Cristóbal," I say rebelliously, and he immediately cuts me short. "Control yourself, boy. Don't try to misuse your position here."

His words crackle. But controlling myself is precisely what I intend not to do.

His fingers drum a *seguidilla* on the tabletop. As usual, he's looking everywhere else except at me.

"I'm going to dictate to you a letter that I will send from the islands. To my son Diego."

That suits me admirably. I've sharpened the quill—it

168

has twice slipped out of my clumsy fingers without his condescending to notice it—and position the parchment.

"Write the date," he commands, "and the usual."

The usual. That's the sign of the cross before the salutation, at the top, in the center of the letter, which means "in the name of the Savior." In Spain, anyone who doesn't add that to a piece of writing makes himself suspect.

Instead of doing that, I move my quill back to the right, where in Jewish text it would be at the beginning of a line, and write in Hebraic script the beth and the hay—the letters for the beginning of *boruch ha-shem,* praise be to the Lord.

He isn't anywhere near the table. But in one spring he's beside me, as if he intended to pounce on a prey, takes—no, tears—the quill out of my hand, and draws a large, unmistakable sign of the cross in front of the beth hay.

Then he says, "Take another sheet. Or no. Wait. For Diego it can be used that way."

"Your Grace Don Cristóbal Colón," I say. "You are a Jew in your flesh. When did *you* have yourself baptized?"

Never in my life have I received such a box on the ear. I've always thought that "seeing stars" was meant only in a metaphoric sense, and for a moment I think I've lost the hearing in one ear, while he goes to the window and makes sure that no one is in the vicinity. But I don't intend to give up.

"I can put one and one together, as you well know," I go on, blinking to keep back the tears the blow has brought to my eyes. "The most powerful Converso in this country, Don Luis de Santángel, gave the money from his private purse to put together the ships and crews—ships on which someone with a recommendation from Abrabanel and a purse of gold could hire on, if he were lucky. A cousin to Santángel is voyaging on this flagship, and he is not the only Converso, as you know better than I. What kind of a ship is it that has no priest on board but has an interpreter of Hebrew? And what are you seeking to discover in the Indies, Don Cristóbal? Where do our Indies lie, to which we are sailing on a southern course, although it is said that we are seeking the East by voyaging west?"

I'm out of breath after my long speech. He sits opposite me, his head supported in both hands. I can't see his face, only the white hair. It is quiet, and I feel my cheek flaming where it now certainly bears the mark of his hand. The crew will have something else to laugh about at my expense.

"Very well," he says with a sigh. He lifts his face from his hands and looks at me, and I hold the stare of the gray, sparkling eyes. "Very well, nosy know-it-all. I've let you have too deep a look into certain things, which was certainly a mistake on my part. But now I clearly owe it to you. You're figuring things out. Some you have right. Others not."

I say nothing. He continues.

"First," he says seriously, "you should know that I am committed to Our Lord and Savior Jesus Christ with all my heart and all my mind, with all my instincts, with good and bad thoughts, with my body and my soul." He raises the crucifix of his rosary to his lips and kisses it with eyes closed. "As true as I live. Amen."

Now he looks at me.

"Hundreds of years ago, so they say, my family was once persecuted as adherents of the Old Testament and fled from Spain to Lombardy. There, *without* pressure and compulsion, they converted to the Christian faith. Thus, if you wish to put it that way, the Colóns have been Conversos for hundreds of years. But in this family, converting to the new belief never meant forswearing the old. What God promised, his only begotten Son fulfilled through his death on the cross. Only fools can assume that one must scorn the Jewish faith in order to profess the Christian. Jesus Christ has provided Judaism with new life. Therefore, none of my fathers and forefathers thought to forswear the old faith. The Colóns in Genoa and in Lombardy kept the Sabbath holy; they learned the old prayers along with the new ones. They didn't forget where they came from. It's disgraceful to deny one's heritage. Yes, and they had their sons circumcised and baptized at the same time. Old and New Testaments joined. Does that satisfy you, Señor Pedro, who confesses the Lord Jesus only with your lips?"

I nod dumbly. He is a Jew, I think. He can twist it and turn it as he will. According to the law of Moses, he is a Jew. And according to the law of Grand Inquisitor Torquemada as well.

"Then in Portugal and Spain I found out what it means to be a Converso," he continues. "A nothing. However, I found my true friends and helpers among the baptized Jews, as they would also like to be called in their new faith. We recognized each other by the old signs, through which you also have betrayed yourself, Pedro.

"And now the following: In times of persecution hope is greatest. And the belief in salvation. We all read the old writings. Do you know these words, 'Surely the islands shall wait for me, and the trading ships from distant lands first, to bring your children there from afar, together with their silver and gold'?"

"That's in the Prophet Isaiah," I reply, and a smile comes into his eyes.

"And this: 'For behold, I will create a new heaven and a new earth'?"

"Also Isaiah."

"I've studied the prophets. They say the same things as the new writings of the explorers and travelers. God will not abandon the children of the Old Testament. He will try them, but He will not abandon them."

"May I ask questions, Your Grace?"

"That's why you're here," he replies. "Wait a moment." He goes to the door and calls softly into the falling dusk, and almost immediately Diego appears, as if he'd been standing about outside somewhere.

"Bring wine," the admiral commands. "Not the yellow for the crew. The red from Alicante, which doesn't go to one's head. And two glasses. Then see that no one disturbs us. Oh, yes," he adds with a glance at my bandaged hands, "and light the candles."

Chapter Thirteen

"So, ask." He sips wine. The rosary glides through his constantly moving fingers with a soft clicking.

"Your Grace cites the old scriptures and the reports of the world travelers of our time," I begin. "But what do you hope to find, what do the Spanish Jews and Conversos hope to find, when we reach where we're sailing?"

"The lost ten tribes of Israel," he replies quietly. "Opinions are divided over how we will encounter them. Luis de Santángel hopes for Jewish kingdoms. Still others, of whom I am one, expect perhaps not quite so much—nevertheless, cities where Jews live free of overlords and without oppression. Such cities are written of in the books of the famous Marco Polo, who penetrated into the Middle Kingdom. And they were reported by Rabbi Benjamin ibn Jona from Tudela, who also traveled to Asia two hundred years ago. It thus appears to be true, and sailors who've worked their way to the edges of the inhabited world know it, too: Israel will be united with her lost brothers."

"With the ten lost tribes?" I murmur, and I feel as if I've been transported into the stories of the *Thousand and One Nights,* and someone has just said, "Open sesame," and I'm seeing the cave of marvels.

"But you know the writings of the Old Testament," he replies, and there's a trace of impatience in his voice again. "Twelve tribes descended from the twelve sons of the ancestor Jacob. They formed two kingdoms, Judah and Israel. In Judah there lived only two tribes, those of Judah and Benjamin. When the people of this realm were carried off to Babylon, the other ten tribes of Israel were deported and scattered all over the world. Benjamin settled in the lands between the Tigris and the Euphrates. Only Judah returned to its native land. We're all descended from Judah. But the ten tribes of Israel remain missing. Still, the chosen people of the Lord, our God, cannot perish. We have not forgotten them, but they have forgotten us. They live in the lands beyond the sea, where there is freedom, where they are not tolerated guests but are lords and in safety."

I stare at him, and if he now were to tell me that I have wings and I should open them and fly over the ship, I would probably do it. This is how he enchanted them all, with that warm, soft voice, lent an additional charm by the foreign accent, with that mixture of vision and half-truths, of fairy tales that one would like to believe in, of sailors' yarns and dogma. And along with these, his intention to reach the lands on the other side of the ocean. All those ministers and noblemen, those dry clerks and cool financiers—he has something ready for everyone. This strange Genoese sells hopes, whichever type for whomever. Hope for gold and hope for mastery, hope for survival, hope for dignity and freedom, and for the salvation of the faith. And I also am all too ready to believe in him.

"But what moves a statesman and calculator like Santángel to underwrite your plans? Does he think, then, that it's possible to reverse the expulsion or settle the Spanish Jews beyond the sea?"

He shakes his head. "Oh, no," he says, letting his fingers run around the edge of the wineglass. "That would be much too expensive a business. Whatever he does, Santángel doesn't invest to lose! He hopes for a great deal of profit from this undertaking. But certainly he thinks that with the help of my discoveries the edict might be repealed over the course of time, or at least be loosened."

"How? I don't understand, Your Grace."

"Do you remember the sultan's ambassadors a couple of years ago? Oh, of course not. You were still a child. Churchmen from Jerusalem met with high priests and dignitaries of Islam. Then they explained to Her Majesty

Isabella that if the aggression against the Moors did not stop, the sultan would undertake countermeasures against the Christians in Syria and Palestine. After that the war was stopped."

"So you think—"

"Not I. Santángel and many well-known Conversos think that the Jewish kings on the other side of the sea, if there actually are any, can be a support for the Jews here. That they will protest. That they will have to be reckoned with before anyone undertakes anything against the Jews here in the future. In short, that we will enjoy protection."

Merchant of hopes. Merchant of dreams. Carrying out his plans partly depends on those who are persecuted and threatened, on those whose future is uncertain. For a moment I think that he'd have sold his story, with the appropriate changes, to the Grand Turk if he could have been made to give the admiral ships. . . . Genoese gambler.

But I see his eyes leave me and look just beside me or beyond me for what he is seeking. And now his hands, too, those ever-moving hands, are there, helping him talk. "I know it. Intuition and experience are my navigators; the Holy Ghost sits in the ship's lookout. God wills that I get there. God wills that we possess the world, His world, as a whole, and not only a piece of it. He has created it that we may praise Him. If we already praise Him for the all too insufficient part that we know, how great will be the flame of our veneration when we see the whole thing before us. Gold, treasures of the earth, countless souls who await the blessings of religion—"

"Through baptism?" I interrupt, and he says, as if all he has to do is wave it away, "We have no priests on board the ship."

Who should be more ready to follow him than I? He is giving me a gala performance of his magic lantern, which he's made shimmer before princes and kings, and still I sit with doubt in my heart. Where are we sailing?

"Don Cristóbal," I say. "Permit me . . . are we looking for the Indies? We're not sailing west."

"*We are sailing to the Indies,*" he says with emphasis. "This I aver with all my power. Just as you insist that you are Pedro." And he adds, "But I will find not only the Indies. There are other kingdoms, I think, far to the west, immeasurable, unimaginably large. And they have nothing to do with the Middle Kingdom and the Great Khan." He's referring to Their Majesties' letter, which I read to our listener at the wall of the *toldilla* days ago.

I tuck away that remark about my name. It's not about me.

"But who's suggesting this course to you?" I continue stubbornly. "Has an angel of the Lord appeared to you in a dream to tell you that you must first sail south? You speak of intuition and experience. What have you experienced, *señor almirante,* that others don't know? You know this business as no one else does. I don't believe that you're sailing into the blue. You know more than others, and so you've convinced those who are worth convincing."

He looks past me.

"*Señor,*" I say, lowering my voice to a whisper, "was someone there before you?" It's like taking a testing step in the dark. But obviously I hit the mark.

"Yes. Actually, yes," he says, turning his head away. "How you press me, Pedro! They lost an inquisitor in you!"

I cringe. He shouldn't say things like that. He pours himself some more wine and forgets me.

"Yes, there's a map. Am I a fool? Someone was there. I am sailing according to those notations. I'm the only person who has them. Santángel has seen them, and the fathers of the cloister La Rábida, when it was essential to convince them."

"And Their Majesties?"

He bursts out laughing. "Do you think Their Majesties understand anything about sea charts? As much as a donkey does about the ABCs! Ferdinand never trusted me and still doesn't to this day. Isabella— with her, proof isn't necessary. She's a woman, and generally women are quick to believe me."

It sounds condescending, and I can't help lifting my head, but I run right into the broadside of his glance, a barrage of fire. "Now at last I know what Don Pedro Gutiérrez is looking for," I say, and he answers, "Yes, now you know. But we are seeking the Indies. Nothing else."

"Nothing else," I reply, and I take up my wine and drink it down in one long gulp.

It's quiet outside. But someone on this ship begins to sing, softly. It sounds out of place. I pull myself together. Pedro, you've received information. More you will not get ... if you even really have learned anything true or just another version—

"Well, run out of questions?"

"No," I say, and pull all my courage together. "You spoke of the traditions in your family, Don Cristóbal. Your son—"

"My sons," he corrects me. "There are several, even if they don't all come from my wife, whom God has called to Him. No, Pedro. I haven't carried on the tradition of combining the two religions any further. We live in Spain." His voice grows soft. "Gog in the land of Magog, do you know that? The last days. The demon is already living among us. I must protect them."

Now, finally, he is near me, and I sense his sadness and that at this moment he is being truthful.

"Permit me to kiss your hand," I whisper, standing up.

"Leave that," he says, and he also stands up. "Go sleep."

"I am Your Grace's servant."

"Yes, that you certainly are," he replies, turning away

from me to look at the stars through the window of the *toldilla*.

I'm already standing in the doorway. With a deep sigh I say, "There's something else Your Grace should perhaps know. Someone pushed me overboard last night."

No reaction.

"They thought I couldn't swim."

"But you can, and you were able to save yourself, since you were sitting there in front of me today," he says, as if we were talking about a third person. He doesn't turn around. "Pedro, I can't watch over you. You must do that yourself."

"I thought it would interest Your Grace to know that there's a murderer on the *Santa María*."

"No murder has taken place yet, so there is no murderer. The Lord has His hand over even the lost souls. And I think there are many of those on these ships."

Outside the voice sings, *"Qu' es di te, desconsolado?"* Whither goest thou, disconsolate one?

It's cool outside now.

Chapter Fourteen

*H*alf the ship knows that Pedro was drinking wine in the admiral's cabin last evening. And whoever doesn't know it yet gets to hear it when the marks on my face are noticed. He who dines with the gentry must have a long spoon. And more witticisms of that sort. What did I do, then? "I tipped over the inkwell," I say. It's the best I can come up with.

They are amused. "Well, Pedrito, he really landed one! The admiral's a good swordsman, it appears!"

I gather that evidently a man rises in the estimation of his inferiors on this ship when he's able to properly wallop them.

As I swab the deck I steal a glance into the mirror of the pail. My cheek is blue, shading into green. And yesterday evening I even begged to kiss that hand. Well, thank you.

Maestro Bernal changes the bandages on my hands and is pleased at how quickly everything is healing. "Do I still have to wear them?" I ask. "They make fun of me."

He hesitates. "Because of possible work on the ropes," he says. "At least one more day." Then he looks askance at my face and murmurs, "He shouldn't do that."

"He won't do it again," I say with more confidence than is perhaps warranted.

We're now in the third day of the calm, but toward noon the air starts moving, as it did the evening I put the salve on the admiral, and this time it's not a deceptive breeze. The wind freshens. As he predicted, from the opposite direction. There is feverish activity on the *Santa María* to make her ready to sail.

I have duty in the *bitácula*, the compass house. By this time, Pero Niño, the navigator, has also realized that I understand something about navigation and has me call out the course changes.

So I'm there to hear the dispute the admiral and Juan de la Cosa have at the signal fire. Evidently the Basque is refusing to send over to the *Pinta* the very information the admiral had already conveyed to Cristóbal Quintero shortly before the beginning of the calm.

"But *almirante,* with all respect, that goes counter to the rules of Christian seafaring!" cries the owner.

Columbus is already red in the face. "Don't try to lecture me on the rules of Christian seafaring, Señor de la Cosa! Do as I ordered!"

Now Niño turns the tiller over to one of the sailors in order to join in the argument. The navigator is a quiet man of middle age, generally well regarded because of his love of justice, and an outstanding sailor. For this reason Their Majesties have given him the title *pilato mayor* of Castile. Also he is one of the few people who were ready to make the voyage without the "good persuasion" of the Pinzóns.

"Don Cristóbal, the captain is right!" he says placatingly. "It's not the custom, as you very well know yourself, to leave a disabled ship in the lurch when one is sailing in a fleet. I suggest sending the *Niña* ahead to Gran Canaria to get help for the *Pinta*. The flagship should stay here."

"I have not asked you for suggestions, *señor pilato*! This fleet is under my command and not that of a consortium of amateurs!"

"Amateurs? Do you think, in all seriousness, *almirante*, that we are worse seamen than—than others?"

"I do not intend to discuss your qualifications! Carry out the orders!"

"It is against custom, *almirante*. We ask you only to consider—" That's Juan de la Cosa again. But he gets no further.

"One more word, gentlemen, and I will call Señor de

Arana to put you in irons as mutineers and hand you over to the *gobernadora* of the island! Will you obey or not?"

The *pilato mayor* places a soothing hand on the owner's arm, although you can see that he's seething. "As you command, *almirante*," he says tersely. "We will leave the *Pinta* behind with orders to get to the harbor of Gran Canaria under her own power. The flagship and the *Niña* will set course for Gomera." He and Columbus measure each other with their eyes. Then the admiral turns on his heel and goes to the aftercastle with a hail of Italian curse words.

The two officers say nothing. There is not even one of the usual maledictions on the damned Genoese.

I LEARN ONLY THAT EVENING, when I have a little time off, how very much he's offended everyone with this decision.

We've sweated and strained the entire day, for sailing against the wind isn't so easy, and the clumsy *Santa María* bucks like a horse that's trying to throw off its rider. I'm glad I've followed Maestro Bernal's advice and am still wearing the bandages, or my palms would probably be raw meat.

In front of us the *Niña* describes her marvelously graceful dance steps, and behind us the groggily rolling *Pinta* is soon lost on the horizon.

The admiral himself directs the operations. It's

the first time he's given his orders directly and not transmitted them through the owner. Obviously he means to discipline de la Cosa for his insubordination by ignoring him.

With legs spread, hair flying in the wind, he stands on the bridge, looking anything but dignified—more like an animal about to spring. Nothing escapes him. He appears to foresee every situation and often calls out the course instructions before the compass is read, taking advantage of the capricious wind again and again.

The crew is panting with exhaustion, cursing, screaming. One begins to cry, and some are also affected by *mal de mer* with this unpredictable up and down.

But there's a cry of jubilation toward evening when we catch up with the nimble little *Niña* and are gliding side by side with her in the path of the setting sun.

The admiral has the sails reefed and heaves to for the night. Under such uncertain wind conditions, nighttime sailing is not possible, unless we want to sail way off course. We've kept seeing the tips of the island's mountains appear on the horizon and then losing them again. Next to God, probably only that Genoese knows where we've been dancing around today—at least so think the men who drop exhausted in their tracks, with an extra ration of wine in their gullets after this day.

"Viva el almirante!" calls Chachu at the end of today's passage, pulling off his red wool cap, and the crew joins

in. The mate might be satisfied. But now they let loose, and their tongues wag.

"I call that sailing!" says one of the Basques. But another growls, "I call that scramming. No decent seaman leaves a damaged ship behind."

Meanwhile it's gotten so dark that I can't tell the gentlemen of the foreship apart from those of the aftership.

"Well, if Captain Pinzón is as good as he says he is, he can get to Gran Canaria alone," another pipes up, but he earns a protest. "That's not what it's about, Paco! That's simply not seamen's custom. Something like that doesn't bring luck. The *señores* de la Cosa and Niño, they didn't want to do it. But the Genoese, he yelled at them. You were right there, Pedrito, right?"

"I didn't hear a word," I say firmly, and they laugh.

"What's the matter with you, then?" growls another voice, which could be García's. "We're on course. We're on course, and it's good."

They snuffle and belch. Then another one gets going. "Yes, but that's still the question, who's on course here. As far as I understand, we're sailing toward Gomera. But I don't want to go to Gomera. I want to go to gold country. All right, all right. First some more fresh water, fresh meat. Women one more time. But that's all to be had in Gran Canaria, in the harbor, at the shipyard. Who of us has to go to Gomera?"

For a while there's silence, and then the same voice

says, "Our admiral has to go to Gomera. He has to stick his stopper in a pot they say holds pepper mixed with honey."

Someone whistles. "You mean La Cazadora?"

There's shifting among the men. "Exactly. La Cazadora, the huntress. The governor of the Canary Islands. That must be some woman! Even King Ferdinand was supposed to be stuck on her!"

"Why's she called the huntress?" I hear myself asking. The men laugh. "Listen to that one! You want to know ahead of time, eh, Pedro? She's called the huntress because she catches men instead of waiting until one of them asks her. She whistles, and the fellows jump."

I repress a laugh in the darkness. Good, more than good, if the men have found a plausible reason for why the course goes southward.

La Cazadora . . . didn't Arana also mention her when I was lying there behind the curtains of the bed, hardly daring to breathe? "The reason has green eyes and black hair," and Alonso with his "witch" . . . Good, they should just believe it. No one on this ship knows more than I about what this course means.

Surprisingly, when I leave the circle of men for a moment to look after the sandglass, someone speaks to me. "A few words, Pedro." I turn around. It's Señor Sánchez, the *veedor real,* and it almost seems as though he's been waiting for me. He appears to have lost weight since we've been on board—a chicken can't be slaughtered for him every day—and a blue-black stubble of beard covers his cheeks, so I hardly recognize him except by his lace collar.

"I am at your service, *señor*," I say. He takes me by the arm and leads me into a corner of the bow, where he clearly assumes we won't be overheard.

"I want to warn you, boy," says the great man through his teeth.

I can't believe my ears. Their Majesties' official makes it his business to warn the ship's boy? And about what? "I don't follow Your Grace," I say truthfully.

"Don't pretend to be stupid," replies Sánchez with anger in his voice. "The devil is loose here on board because Their Majesties have seen fit to send a spy along. This gentleman doesn't like a few noses, or, to be more precise, a few cut pricks. And he doesn't like the admiral's course. And you, my boy, you're close to the admiral. You're running the risk of becoming acquainted with a knife if you don't obey him and disclose what you know. I'm still the senior official here on board, and I have powerful friends. I can protect you. I've asked you once to let me know what's going on. Now I'm asking for the second time, and you would be wise to decide to work for me. I'm not ready to do anything for you if you do nothing for me. One can very easily land in the nettles if one doesn't watch out."

"Don Rodrigo," I say anxiously, "I'm only a grummet—what do you want of me?"

His laugh is a snarl. "Grummets who come on board with a recommendation to Escobedo are suspect to me. Don't think you can take me for a fool. The tendencies of this Colón concern me little. He can have as many boys as he wants between his sheets. But I don't see why I shouldn't profit from it."

For a moment I've lost the power to speak. I feel the blood rush to my face in the darkness, and I think of the night I rubbed the admiral's back with balm. . . . It must be true that you aren't unobserved on this ship for a single moment! "I swear by God Almighty," I say with a thick voice, "that I am the admiral's scribe. Nothing else."

"Rather, swear by the saints," says Sánchez sarcastically, "that's the custom with old believers like you and me. I tell you, I don't care about that. What I want from you is this: Inform me about the admiral's conversations with Gutiérrez, so that I can tell others about what he's up to, and all is well. Otherwise . . ."

"I know nothing. I can do nothing for Your Grace," I say. "Why don't you ask him yourself? The admiral, I mean."

"So that dangerous snooper Gutiérrez gets the idea I'm observing him? That would be the worst thing I could do, to call on the admiral in my capacity as royal official."

He looks at me challengingly, but I am silent.

Then he shrugs. "Very well. Then I can do nothing for you, either. Too bad. I'll tell you once more: You have enemies."

And he's gone.

I have something like a lump in my throat when I come back to the others, who joke about where I've been for so long if I didn't just come down from the crapper. I don't want to be a spy for any mighty master. I have only a single master here on board, and that is Christopher Columbus. And what enemies was he talking about? Someone certainly did push me overboard, and the Andalusian boys with Alonso at their head are not exactly my friends—but otherwise? Who would dare to harm me if I stand in the protection of the most powerful man on this voyage? True, he's said to me that I must watch out for myself. Good, I'll do that. Only if he can't stand by me, how does a Rodrigo Sánchez think that he can?

I'm anxious, yes, but I decide to look at the whole thing as an attempt at intimidation by the *veedor real* so that he can get his information through me. No, I won't go along with that. *Basta.*

I'm only that far along in my ruminations when someone squawks out of the darkness, "Pedro to the admiral!"

I stand up, and for some reason I'm angry. The absurd accusation that the admiral wants to do more with his ship's boy than draw charts and read books keeps going around in my head, and it upsets me, though I can't really say why. Let them just think what they want.

THE MEN LAUGH. "Second watch for Pedro! Special watch with wine and ear boxing!" They're more right than they know.

"Where've you been hiding, *per amor di Dio*? Can't you figure out that after a day like this, entries have to be made, so you can't lie around somewhere on your lazy bones?"

My admiral is irritated. Evidently today's matter of his officers' disputing his tactics has upset him more than he wants to show.

The big chart is lying on the table. The second one lies next to it. We've been hopping back and forth like a cricket in the meadow. Yet I see only a single straight line on the paper. Is he now beginning to falsify even his own logs and deceive himself as well?

"Well?" he asks. "How did you like this day?"

I can't understand it. He asks his moses how he liked it that he outsailed the *Niña*! I clench my teeth.

"I understand too little of sailing, Your Grace," I reply. "The crew is of the opinion that you are a great seaman but that it was a mistake to leave the *Pinta* behind."

"Ah," he says sharply. "Since when do you appoint yourself the advocate for the crew and tell me the opinion of the mob?"

"Since I carry the mark of Your Grace's hand on my cheek as I walk around the ship," I say, and immediately I know I've gone too far.

He expels his breath with a hiss. *"Ragazzo impertinente,"* he says in a low voice. He grabs me by the hair and pulls my head back. "You need a lesson, eh?"

I squeeze my eyes tightly shut. Close to panic, I realize that in his violent rage he could shatter my head on the table and break my nose. I say nothing. I'm able to say nothing at all. The air is trapped in my lungs. All I can think of is that soon something somewhere in me is going to hurt very much. Then he lets me go.

I run both my hands over my face and look carefully around at him. Obviously he's just finished crossing himself. Three times, as you're supposed to. His head is sunk.

"Come, get to your work," he says, as if nothing has happened. "Copy this." He intends to show me something. But then he pulls back his hand with its outstretched finger. But I've seen it. It's trembling.

I wait quietly. It would be best if he sent me away.

"I wouldn't be a good chart maker this evening," he says with a little laugh. "We weren't either of us very smart just now, were we, Pedro? Anger is a heavy sin. But I can't tolerate rebelliousness."

He sits down at the table. "Now, what is it?"

"I'm afraid that I'm not a good chart maker tonight, either, may it please you," I say. My voice sounds strange to me.

He nods. "Yes, I understand that. Too bad, there's much to be done."

"I'm ready at any time to serve you, *señor el almirante*," I say. "May I ask you two questions?"

He waves a hand in agreement. "When do you not have questions, Pedro?"

"Why did Your Grace enter a straight course in your personal logbook? It seemed to me that we were sailing in a very complicated line."

"Right," he replies. "But that line isn't important for the entry. I need only our effective course. In reality, it looked something like this today." He pulls a sheet of parchment over and is about to take up the quill, but when he sees that his hand is still trembling, he says angrily, "Well, what's going on?" and presses the palm of his hand firmly on the tabletop for a moment, so firmly that his knuckles turn white. Then he begins, quickly, in a sort of rough sketch, to draw the coordinates of our position and the course sailed by the *Santa María*. He doesn't once refer to the actual reckoning for help. "So," he says, "and from this we develop the mean that's entered there on the chart." Now I must tell him once again how much I admire his skill. He values that, and so I do it, although he appears not to be listening at all, and now that he has the quill in his hand, he continues listing some columns of figures. "You can go," he says casually. "Do it tomorrow. Oh, your second question."

"Did Your Grace intend to smash my face on the table?" I ask, and once more I've overstepped the boundary.

He doesn't look at me. "Eh? What? Hey, what's that? I just intended to slap you one, *mozo*." He says it roughly, in the inflections of a port bar, and it sounds false. He probably doesn't know himself. And above all, he doesn't care.

Chapter Fifteen

In the single turn of the sandglass I've been away, the crew's mood has heated up, and none other than La Cazadora is to blame. My return isn't really noticed at all, very much to my relief, so I can lie down behind the mast and try not to overhear.

In the half year I've been tramping around on the highways of Castile I've had to hear and see things that a proper Jewish girl wouldn't hear in her whole life. My ears have gotten callused, so to speak. (Like my soul.) And I can't always avert my eyes, either. At least that's easier for me this time. It's dark, after all, and the men are also just at the stage where they're feeding their imaginations with words. From time to time the wind brings me a few scraps that I could gladly do without. One of them must have seen this legendary governor once.

"Tits like Monte Perdu!" I hear. (That must be one of the Basques.) "Lace trimming around the neck, you understand, and under it naked flesh right down to the buds!" The men groan. I wish I had something to stop up my ears. Breasts like Monte Perdu! I sneak my hand under my shirt. I probably can't ever expect anything like that, not even in ten years.

I gather myself up quietly, to go below deck to spend the rest of the night there, as much as it stinks so terribly, among the rats and the flour sacks.

Only I don't get that far. A hand closes around my neck and someone asks me softly, "Well, boy, how'd you like the bath day before yesterday?"

I don't even try to turn around. The hand is like a vise. My heart is skipping against my ribs in irregular leaps. I don't even think of the words of a prayer. A knife, I think numbly. The next thing is a knife. And then something splashes into the water. This time a thorough job. This time it won't come up again.

But it doesn't happen. For horrible, endless seconds nothing happens, except that someone is holding me and breathing down my neck and in the background the rats are rushing around in the ship and leaping and squeaking.

Finally I say as energetically as possible, although my voice betrays me, "Thank you for the inquiry. Was it you that helped me over, *señor*?"

There's a laugh behind me. "No, *mozo*. I only watched.

Pure accident. Not too clumsy, how you got yourself out of it."

Apparently someone doesn't intend for me to be alive tonight. I listen to the voice—do I know the speaker? In any case, it certainly isn't one of the Basques. "How can I serve you, *señor*?" I ask, and when there's no answer, I carefully add, "Would you let go of my neck? It hurts very much, and I'm certainly not going to run away."

To my amazement, he does. I turn around cautiously. I look at the man in the uncertain light of the deck lantern falling through the hatch. I don't know him. It's one of the crew I haven't seen yet. Some Juan, Luis, Diego, or other who climbs the rigging and hangs on the ropes. He doesn't look unfriendly. The fear is still in my very bones. My knees are weak. Nevertheless, I repeat, "How can I serve you?" He laughs. "No, you can't serve me. But there are a few people you can serve. They want to talk to you."

"Right now?" I ask. "Couldn't they find any other way to offer me their invitation?"

The terrible fear is slowly turning to rage. As if I hadn't already been through enough here on this tub!

"Oh, well," he says, "this just happened. No, not right now. We wanted to play a little trick on you, too."

"We? Who's we?"

"Us Andalusians. You hang around with the Basques too much, y'know. You shouldn't do that. You can't trust the Basques out of your sight. They stick together, don't let anyone in. That García always gives to the Basques first, and always the biggest pieces in the pot."

I listen. Sometime he will have to get to the point.

"Think about that."

"Tell your Andalusians that you've delivered their message"—I hesitate—"that they like me."

He growls. "Not too cheeky, boy, eh? I can do other things, too."

I don't doubt it.

"So," he begins, "if the admiral sails again tomorrow and doesn't need you, you should go to our gentlemen passengers and report to the don from the court. The tall one."

"Gutiérrez?"

"Right. Señor Gutiérrez."

Aha. Now it's out. That's where the wind is blowing. That must be what Sánchez meant.

"Good," I say. "Understood. I only wonder why that majordomo couldn't tell me that. Or Señor Gutiérrez himself, all nice and normal, by day and not below deck and without grabbing a person by the back of the neck."

The fellow shrugs. "Might just be," he offers with a grin, "that it's not only the Andalusian seafolk who want to scare you a little."

I nod. "Yes, it might just be. But what happens if the admiral doesn't sail tomorrow?"

"Then they'll certainly think of something else." He may be right there.

* * *

I CAN'T FALL ASLEEP FOR AGES. The fear I'm laboring under hits me in the stomach, and I have to run to the necessary three times. Luckily the men on watch and the others who aren't sleeping are still busy with their favorite theme: women! They don't pay any attention to me.

I feel like a mouse in a trap. If I go to García, I make the Andalusians angry at me; if I play up to the Andalusians, the Basques are against me. They can all harass me, and then there's still my shipmate Alonso and his peon friends, whose truce will come to an end, at the latest, when I refuse to carry out my "sacred oath" and steal the amulet for him, or whatever else they want there. Not to mention that interpreter, who for a wonder has so far kept in the background. Now that the eyes of the noble gentlemen, too, have fallen on me—Gutiérrez, Sánchez—it is like being in a mousetrap.

Really, it's only a question of time until someone gets the idea that this grummet deserves a proper thrashing. At the very latest, it's over when they bind me to the mast and tear off my shirt. Then I needn't even tell them on top of it that I'm a Jewess.

And the admiral? "You must look after yourself," he said when I told him that someone tried to kill me. He didn't care enough about the information to turn his eyes away from the stars at the window. The admiral won't protect me. What am I to him against his dream of the lands on the other side of the sea, whether there are Jewish kingdoms there, the Indies, or something entirely different? And maybe he doesn't even want me to be protected at all, who knows? Maybe it's burdensome to him that I've seen and heard so much, and he'd be glad to be rid of me.

The rats are frolicking around in the bilge. I toss my head back and forth, the way the pious Jews do in the synagogue when they pray. But I don't want to transport myself into ecstasy, I just want to fall asleep. And then I want the Lord to perform a miracle. I want to wake up early tomorrow after someone has just called *"Tierra a la vista!"*—land in sight. And this land must be the Indies. Under no circumstances Gomera.

But that is, of course, a very silly wish.

THE WEATHER THIS MORNING is really the same. But the admiral doesn't sail today. So our gentlemen passengers must think of something else in order to arrange to talk with me.

And then they do just that. Diego de Arana, the "relation" of the admiral, immediately sends to ask to "borrow" me, since he has a few calculations to work up that he doesn't wish to bother Don Escobedo with. And since space is tight on board, he also asks that the *toldilla* be placed at his disposal for half an hour! He is utterly shameless.

"He can calculate like a wizard," says my admiral. "I

know that. He doesn't need you for that. The whole thing is as transparent as glass. He intends to suborn you on the spot to steal my charts for him. Keep your ears open, Pedro, and report to me down to the smallest detail."

The half hour—one turn of the sandglass—is granted. The admiral has to take care of sailing maneuvers anyway.

Yes, I am ready to do everything for my master, be he kind or unkind. But it turns out differently.

As soon as I see the two of them sitting there next to each other at the table, the *señores* provost and courtier, severe anxiety overwhelms me. They're not even trying to act as if they want me to write something or to calculate.

"Sit down over there, Pedro," Arana says, and points to the chest in which the admiral's things are secured. I obey the command and am just about to open my mouth and ask for the gentlemen's orders as he continues, "Make the sign of the cross and say the Confession of Faith."

I begin with numb lips to say the Confiteor, and my hand shakes as I make the sign of the cross.

But Gutiérrez breaks in after the first few words and says, "I think we don't need that, *señor alguacil*. He's confessing it with his mouth but not with his heart."

Arana nods. "There are indications that you are only the pretense of a Christian, Pedro. An honorable man, himself a new Christian but of irreproachable orthodoxy, has observed you. During the second day of our voyage, when you were among those being seasick, you said a Jewish prayer."

"I cannot speak a word of that language," I say. "I come from an orthodox Christian family and—"

"Who said you spoke the language? Only a Jewish prayer was mentioned."

It's over. They have me. Fearing discovery, the interpreter has turned the lance around.

"*Señores!*" I say. "I swear by the Holy Virgin and all the saints that that man is lying. He himself spoke in that language and—"

"So you admit that someone heard you and, it appears, you even know who heard you."

"It's a slander," I say.

They look at each other.

Arana puts on a grin. "Yes, it always sounds like this when false Christians defend themselves, Pedro! There's no representative of the Holy Inquisition on this ship, that you know very well, and some others know that. Heretics have sneaked on board. As provost, I must keep my eye on everything. There is information against you. We'll see what we do with you at Gomera."

"The Holy Inquisition is not in the islands," I say, "and I am an orthodox Christian. Your informant is lying."

Now Gutiérrez chimes in, with his nasal inflection, "You certainly know frightfully precisely where the defenders of the faith are and where they are not.

Possibly heretics are not being judged there yet. But that will soon change. I am very closely connected with the Santa Hermandad. My voyage has a reason, you can believe me about that, boy."

I am silent, apparently unimpressed.

Again the two gentlemen look at each other.

Arana makes a gesture as if to say: Well, then, we must pluck another string. He takes over again. "Naturally we must inform the crew that someone here has unmasked you as a heretic. We owe that to the pious souls."

They've won. Unthinkable, what the crew would do to me if my "heresy" were made public! I drop my head. "How can I deserve the pity of the distinguished gentlemen?" I say with lowered head. "My lot on this ship would be deplorable, for in their pious zeal, many would take the suspicion for proven godlessness."

"You've spoken very prettily, very sensibly," that contemptible Arana praises me. "There is indeed something you can do that would shift your zeal for the true faith into a proper light and render a service to the Brotherhood."

My heart hammers in my chest. I feel each beat all the way up in my temples.

"I'm willing, Your Grace." Of course I'm willing.

Now Gutiérrez is talking. "We have reason to assume that the admiral is withholding something from Their Majesties. The power and the resources of both Castiles are invested in this undertaking"—and the maravedis of

Santángel, I think—"and if dishonesty were involved, Their Majesties must learn about it. One can still call the voyage back from the islands. I would have the full power. You had a look into Don Cristóbal's papers. Have you seen a chart that is kept secret?"

I stiffen. "I have not seen it, Your Grace," I gasp out.

"Have you heard him speak about it?"

I press my lips together, shake my head. "I don't know, sir."

"You don't know. Although you know so much otherwise. That is not good. It is very necessary that we get to see this chart."

I nod.

"Have you the key to this chest?"

I remain silent.

Arana has stood up and is inspecting the strongbox. The second key is sticking in the lock. It's the one that the admiral usually keeps in his pocket. The first key is very much smaller and more delicate. "Do you know where the admiral keeps the other key? Answer!" he commands me.

"Yes. It hangs around his neck," I say softly.

The two exchange looks again. "You will find a way to get both keys. You will give this chart into our hands. It doesn't matter how. But it must happen before we reach the islands. You understand us, boy, don't you?"

I understand.

Then they're gone, and I crouch there, clutching the

edges of the chest on which I'm sitting. There's no way I can stand up now.

Farewell, Jewish kingdoms. Farewell, freedom beyond the sea. Good luck to all those who reach them—and I hope he will sail there in spite of everything. I, however, will not be among those who arrive. They've caught me, just when I was believing that I'd escaped. I can only hope that they keep their word and just charge me in Gomera, not surrender me to the men of the *Santa María*. If I get to Gomera, I might perhaps have a chance to flee. So long as they don't take me on land in irons, I might perhaps be able to get away. There will be enough confusion in a landing like that. Perhaps they won't watch the boys. Perhaps.

And for the sake of this "perhaps" I am now getting ready to betray my admiral. I, the daughter of Rabbi Judah. A traitor. A thief.

It's very simple. From the moment when a member of the Brotherhood or the Inquisition demands that a Marrano make the sign of the cross and say the Confession of Faith, the judgment is already spoken. Suspicion is judgment. Accusation is proof. A trap snaps shut. And in my panicked fear I also gave the correct wrong answers.

I've fallen into paralysis, like a young animal grabbed by the neck by a wolf and carried off. It's still not dead yet. It could perhaps run away. But it's given up. I've seen what I have seen.

I know how hair frizzles before the flames spread to it; I know how skin blisters and explodes, how it turns black, and how fat and fluids run down. I've smelled it. I know how they scream and howl, how they turn into torches.

I have more fear than is good for me. I have so much more fear than is necessary for survival. These are not the times for heroes.

I know only one thing: I do not want to burn.

Yes, I will do everything. Everything, *señores*.

I HAVE A LITTLE TIME to collect myself, and then he comes in, his hair blown by the wind, his face reddened, not with one of his outbreaks of rage but, rather, with happy expectation.

"We're lying well before the wind. The ship is a cow, of course, but she's one the men can force to act like a horse. Get down off my chest, help me off with my doublet, and stop looking as though a mythical beast has crossed your path."

"Your Grace hasn't condescended to notice my expression before."

"You're not able to evaluate that, Pedro, I think. After the talk with the two ... gentlemen, I'm looking more carefully. They want the map from you, am I right?"

"Yes, Your Grace."

"And? Did you promise it to them?"

He doesn't wait for my answer but takes the key from

his neck to unlock the strongbox, and I mechanically consider how I can get possession of it. "Lay aside your sour face and do your tasks as I have taught you. First that of yesterday, then that of today. I will work on. Heavens, boy, why do you need so long to sharpen a quill? No, not that one, give me the other. I don't like to work with a broad quill, as you should know by this time."

Somehow I accomplish my tasks, mechanically saying, *Sí, señor,* or *No, señor,* when he asks me something. It's as if I weren't here at all, like a body without a soul, like a ghost, a golem, who does what is demanded of him, a creature of clay who responds to orders. The flames that have haunted me all these weeks, the smell of burned flesh, the piles of kindling, and the screams that I'd banished down deep in the pit of memories—they're there again. And now I'm there and am paying my price.

The Rabbi Judah Marchadi, my father—blessed be the memory of the righteous—said once, "In bad times there is a great demand for bad men."

I know. I'm going to be able to count myself among them.

Chapter Sixteen

A cat has nine lives, they say. I always repeated that up until the moment when they stoned my cat to death and threw her over the wall into our garden. The cat hadn't done anything to anyone. It was only because she was the cat of a Jewish girl. For that she lost even her ninth life.

Somehow I seem to be related to this animal. Yesterday I was still thinking that now I'd caught up with my cat and it was the ninth life's turn. But perhaps it was only the eighth, or the seventh.

Yesterday I was ready to say kaddish for myself. Today I'm again looking for a way out, be it ever so small.

Just the fact that we're still crossing in front of the islands, that thus one day, perhaps two days can be gained, fills me with hope. I'm still here. In the homilies it says,

"A living dog is better than a dead lion." But of course the best of all would be a living lion.

At least I have the feeling that the paralysis that took hold of me in the face of danger is gone. True, on a ship there's even less chance to run away than otherwise. But there are many gradations between running away and sitting there like a lamb waiting for the butcher's knife.

Yes, I feel like an animal. An animal that is being hunted. An animal that is fighting to escape.

The story is coming together bit by bit. What did my dumb "friend" Alonso say when he signed me up for stealing the amulet in Latin? "He doesn't know that language." Not *that* language—he meant the interpreter, obviously. That was his first attempt to get rid of me. But that wouldn't take place until Gomera and would also be too uncertain. Then he got one of the crew—perhaps a trembling Converso, like himself—to push me to a watery death. That I could swim and save myself was his bad luck.

God of righteousness, what sort of fear must he have, Luis de Torres, hired because he could deal in the right language in the Jewish kingdoms? What sort of fear must he have that he would let the trap close on a little ship's boy! What did they do to him? It must have been even worse than what they could inflict upon a certain Esther Marchadi.

All at once I know who it is on this ship I must speak with. Not him whose ocean eyes I can no longer meet for shame, however much I might wish to. Ah, so very much. No, the threefold murderer of the grummet Pedro, the man who suffers from a fear like mine—I must confide in him, must get him to listen to me. To him I can be open now. Now, when it's all over for me, when hope has shrunk down to a grain. Right down to a grain.

I FIND HIM AT THE BEGINNING of the second watch, when I've finished my work. He's sitting up on the after-castle on a chest, with a book on his knees over which he looks out into empty space without reading. I look over his shoulder and see foreign characters; it must be Chaldean, a language I don't know.

"Praise be to the Lord, Señor de Torres," I say to him in Hebrew. "My name is Pedro. Why do you desire my death?"

He jerks around, and his already pale face appears to turn a shade paler in the shadow of the sails in which he is sitting.

"*No entiendo nada*"—I don't understand anything!—he says in Castilian. His eyes are wide.

"But *señor*, how can you not understand the language in which you are supposed to interpret on the other side of the ocean?" I ask, and I crouch down on the deck in front of him. It is very close here. He can't end the discussion by jumping up and running away without shoving me aside first. "I'll call the provost," he says. "I will not allow you to annoy me. Be off!"

He has snapped his book shut and is clutching it tightly. "Señor de Torres!" I say, still using our mother tongue. "Please listen to me; it won't even take half a turn of the sandglass. It was my fault. I should have confided in you immediately after I heard you praying. I should have given myself into your hands—but perhaps you wouldn't have been ready to listen to me. I am Esther Marchadi, the daughter of a rabbi of Córdoba."

His mouth contorts into a smile. "Don't try to hoodwink me, boy! Leave me in peace!"

"You don't really want me to undress here and prove it," I reply, and I have to laugh over us two poor anxious animals, not ready to believe each other. "I *cannot* harm you, Señor de Torres. I could never harm you and don't want to. But now you have thoroughly seen to that. The day after tomorrow, at the latest, we'll reach Gomera. Then one way or the other I'm off the ship. Either they declare me a heretic or, if I succeed in satisfying Señor Gutiérrez, I must go with the grummet Alonso and steal something from a church, whereby it's as inevitable that I'll be caught as that you're sitting there in front of me. Why did you set so many traps for me, *señor*? Wouldn't one have been enough? And then why did you have to have me thrown overboard, too?"

He moves his lips soundlessly. Finally he murmurs, "The last just happened. Because they'd heard that you can't swim . . ."

"It would certainly have been the simplest," I say, nodding. "And the fastest. The other ways of dying you've sought out for me are much slower. And much more agonizing."

He looks at me, though his eyes don't see me. "But I don't want—all I want is to get over there to the other side."

"I want the very same thing, *señor*."

"It will just be enough that you leave this ship. . . ."

"That I will do with certainty, *señor*," I reply. "That is provided for. I swear by God our Father that I did not intend to reveal your secret. It's my secret, too, after all. Why ever did you assume that I could do something to you, a little ship's boy against a man like you?"

"You're always sitting with the admiral," he murmurs. "One never knows . . ." He never finishes any sentence. "Is it true that you are a woman?"

"No," I say, standing up. "That was only a joke. I am nothing at all anymore. I am someone who hasn't long to live. Am I the only one, Señor de Torres, who has been sacrificed in order to save you? Or were there others, too?"

He says nothing, just looks straight ahead. Why am I still talking with this man; what do I really want from him? That he feel guilty? He'll do that anyway. That we, two victims as we are, feel something like brotherhood? He has only fear, and he will until I'm finally gone.

Somehow I thought that we'd sit together and tell our stories. Something laughable like that. The stories of people who must hide, conceal, lie, who are in flight and are pursued—like one another the way one egg is like another, horribly boring.

"I hope that you make it, Señor de Torres," I say. "And that you can live with what you have done, wherever you arrive."

I receive no answer. I didn't expect one, either.

Perhaps there's still a way out for me.

As I go toward the passengers' quarters, I feel like a fox that the hounds have chased into its den and that rushes from one exit to another, only to find out that a hunter is waiting at each one.

The gentlemen's majordomo listens with a stony face to what I say: Might I speak with Señor Sánchez on a pressing matter? Then he disappears inside.

I wait. I wait, it seems to me, endlessly. Then the man comes out, closes the door behind him, and says, "The *veedor real* is not available to speak with you today or at any other time, boy. I am to say to you furthermore: It's too late now."

I slink away, head hanging. Did I expect anything else? When one sees that a horse is pulling a stranger's cart, why should one care if it's beaten? The *veedor real* has already made his own arrangements with his opponents. Pedro is done for. Pedro is bound to die.

* * *

I perform my work in the *toldilla* as well as I can, but I'm so monosyllabic that the admiral inquires what's wrong with me—I haven't asked anything at all today.

"I'm sad, Your Grace," I say.

"You're moody, Pedro," he corrects me. "Moody like a female. I think you're holding it against me that I've handled you firmly now and again. That was for your own good."

That was because you can't control yourself, I think, saying nothing. All the time I'm racking my brains trying to think how I can get the key to the chest.

Key number two is almost always in the lock. But number one hangs around the neck of Christopher Columbus and as far as I've seen, he takes it off only to sleep—then he puts it under his pillow. But when does the admiral sleep? And how shall I do it? Insert myself into the cabin here and wait, until . . . ? No, nothing will come of that. Sometimes I'm on the point of telling him about the whole thing and asking him to help me. To let him come up with something. We could work together to dupe Señor Gutiérrez, perhaps by preparing a fake chart. But of course that's madness. Why should he take part in such jokes? It's like asking a lion to play with a ball of yarn.

Tonight I can't find a place to sleep. It seems to me as if they've all doubled and tripled themselves, these stinking fellows—or is it just that I have no desire to be anywhere near them?

Finally I go to the sandglass. I was first trusted on this ship with the sandglass. Helping me get over the jumble and disorder of the first days on board and to divide up the voyage that lies before me, the sandglass is almost a friend. We probably won't have much more to do with each other now. It seems my time is running out. I tell the very astonished peon who has the watch that I'm volunteering to relieve him, and he is of course happy to find somewhere to snooze—over there where I can't find a place for myself. In the gray of the morning, amid the chatter of the crew changing watches, I find a corner where I can slide down for an eyeful of sleep. And I probably shouldn't be indulging in too much of that any longer, either. The admiral's advice to decrease my need for sleep was absolutely right. Someone who has no expectation of remaining alive shouldn't be wasting his time.

AND THEN IT LOOKS as though I might be lucky. No, it has nothing to do with the hand of the Lord. Since when does the God of righteousness encourage such villainy as I intend to perform? This is probably the hand of that fickle Dame Fortune, who in the songs they sing at court is always holding the reins.

We still keep tacking back and forth, but Gomera, may the Lord curse it, comes ever closer. And then the admiral orders a bath.

Jumping into the sea once in a while because it's so warm—all right. But a bath is as good as heresy. One does not bathe. In Christian circles, bathing is not considered decent. It's already caused a stir that Don Cristóbal has himself shaved every day. He's the only one in this fleet. And now this. García has to warm a tub of water, so somewhere amidships a cask is placed behind a screen of sailcloth and filled with seawater.

I'm very glad I'm not bidden to this ceremony—that's all I'd need now. That the admiral wants to be alone behind his screen nobody understands so well as I, I who know him. At least in certain respects.

The men are completely beside themselves. The purpose of this extravagance is utterly clear to them. To me, too, incidentally. La Cazadora! "He wants to lie between her sheets smelling like a Persian garden!" they gossip rapturously. And "If he's as good in bed as he is at sailing, the *gobernadora* is to be congratulated!"

Meanwhile, my only question is whether he climbs into the tub wearing a crucifix and a key around his neck. It's at least improbable. So it's now or never.

Scarcely has my admiral disappeared in the direction of his bathtub when I've slipped into the *toldilla*. That doesn't seem unusual to anyone. I go in and out of there at all kinds of odd hours, after all. Who knows what sort of a job he's given me?

Key number two is in the lock. Key number one lies

beside his things on the stool. It hangs on the chain with the cross and is still warm from his body. May God forgive me for betraying the man I love.

I turn the keys in the locks and open the chest. Books. Books. Sealed documents. The letter to the Great Khan. The letters of recommendation. His personal logbook. Letters. Letters. Agreements with the signature of the great Santángel. Toscanelli's map, that entirely illegal document copied from the archives of the Portuguese crown. Still more forgeries—letters from Toscanelli to the admiral, but in his hand, Christopher Columbus's own hand. No chart. Nothing. Nothing at all.

There is no secret chart. There is no sea passage to the Jewish kingdoms.

It's all a trick. We're steering south-southwest merely to get the admiral into the bed of La Cazadora. Arana is right. The reasons for this course are green eyes and black hair.

And I am lost.

Chapter Seventeen

*I*t's not possible to crawl any deeper than I have, down into the belly of the ship, into the dark, into the filth. I've crawled away with my shame and disgrace— and my rage. And as I lie here in the brackish water and tarry pools, the rage increases more and more. It seizes me like a fever, and it makes me drum my fists against the ship's ribs and grind my teeth.

The braggart, the bluffer, the windy Genoese, Don Fantástico! Wrapped in his secrets, which don't exist, tossing around boastful phrases, gold chains and velvet cloaks of deception. Merchant of hopes? Merchant of lies! The admiral of the goatfish and the future governor of the mosquitoes! South-southwest? *Si, señor,* it's not so urgent to get over there—who knows what's in store for us there? Before we find the Indies and the Jewish principalities, we'll make a quick little side trip to La Cazadora. It makes an impression when you arrive with three ships. We'll settle the rest the day after tomorrow.

My life was hanging on that sea chart one way or the other. And now I'm a deceived deceiver. Delivered to the knife like the fish in García's bottomless soup kettle.

With an effort, I stand up. There is no sea chart, gentlemen. They won't believe me. Of course they won't believe me. They'll think I've been as proud as I would gladly have been and as faithful as I really wanted to be. . . . And now I'm only a thief who has found nothing to steal.

All my bones ache, as if I were sick. I clamber over the sacks and barrels of ballast and provisions into the daylight and blink against the sun. It seems to me as though I've spent hours down under there. But the watch hasn't even changed once.

"What a sight you are!" says Chachu to me. "As if you were wallowing around in the bilge water. When's your watch?"

I shrug my shoulders. Always. Not at all. It doesn't matter.

"Well, then, if you pay so little attention to it, you'll certainly have nothing against doing something now instead of lounging around. There's a leak in the bow, we're pumping. Go to the caulker and help him with the tarring. You're thin, you'll fit into corners where grown men can't go."

That's fine with me. At least there I'm hidden away again. The work is hard. It keeps you from thinking.

WHEN I STUMP STIFF-LEGGED onto the deck in the afternoon, the island lies before us, an orb rising steeply out of the sea. Her shores, up to where the green of the forests begins, are black as Hell. I didn't know there was such a thing as black sand. But it fits in perfectly with my frame of mind. To the northeast, a white cloud is sitting almost immobile over the silhouette of the mountains.

We've heaved to. The mood on deck is bustling. We'll run into the harbor tomorrow. The men are going ashore. It may be the last time before the great trip to the lands of gold gets started, the journey into the unknown. For 750 fraudulently plotted leagues to the west, whatever else may be there.

Although it's still early, the *bojito* is already making the rounds. This watch will be relaxed. The *Niña* is anchored nearby, and the men, hands cupped to their mouths, are arranging with men on the other ship to meet this evening. A few have been here before and know the best sailors' bars in San Sebastián.

Someone's found a pair of castanets in his seabag. It's warming up here amidships. The voice that was singing romances in the night is now on *"Niñay Viña,"* a song whose text it would be better not to hear.

Someone taps me on the shoulder. My "mate" Alonso. I'd very nearly forgotten about him.

"See to it that you don't have watch tomorrow night and can give an excuse to your Genoese. But what am I talking about—he'll definitely have something better to do tomorrow night." He gestures descriptively. "We'll go ashore while it's still light. Then to the Iglesia de la Asunción. And then we'll do it."

I shake my head. "No," I say. I've decided, if I still have a choice, on the second way to die. Rather than letting myself be caught as a robber of something that may not even exist, I would rather have it like my father—Lord preserve the memory of the righteous.

"What does that mean, no?" asks Alonso stupidly.

"No means that I'm not doing it," I reply wearily. I want to get this behind me. I don't wish to get myself involved in this nonsense. Amulets and Latin sayings! Absurd.

"Eh?" says my co-grummet slowly. "I'm afraid I heard wrong. You swore an oath, *mozo,* on the life of your mother and the Holy Virgin. Have you forgotten that?"

"The saints were in it, too," I add. "Don't forget the saints!"

"What kind of a bastard are you? Did anyone ever hear of such a thing?"

"Did anyone ever hear that extorted oaths were worth anything?"

"Extorted? Don't make me laugh! Now you're going to find out what extorted is, you stinker!"

We're standing beside the hatch, and while he's been

talking in a conspiratorial whisper, I've been answering perfectly normally. Now he raises his voice. "Hey, Concho, c'mere a minute!" The peon who dropped the cask on my foot appears from behind the edge of the poop and slowly approaches.

"Is something the matter?" he asks menacingly.

"I'll say!" Alonso is getting more and more indignant. "This little swine here doesn't want to keep his promise! He's stubborn! What d'you think of that?"

"Naughty," says Concho. "Very naughty. We'll probably have to do something to persuade him."

He steps back, clearly intending to kick my shin, but I jump to one side and he stumbles, loses his balance, and falls into the hatch. Exactly at this moment the singer in the crew begins the beautiful street song *Yo me soy la morenica,* and Concho's bellow is swallowed up in the rhythmic hand clapping that accompanies it. I can't help myself, I have to laugh. I didn't do anything at all—really, he fell down there all on his own—but it seems to me like the story of David and Goliath.

"Just wait, now you're in for it!" Alonso says, rolling up his sleeves, while his mate down there obviously isn't managing as fast as he'd like.

While the grummet is still measuring me with his eyes, my desperation turns into an anger that floods over me like a wave. I can't run away anyhow. So, then. I duck, and before Alonso knows what's happening, I take a run and butt my head into the pit of his stomach, as if I were a billy goat. He gives a loud bellow, loud enough to attract attention, and the men break off their song. Then he grabs me. I'm only a half-pint, and there are two of them, for Concho has reported in. But I hit wildly around me, bite, scratch, kick. I don't feel the blows I must be taking. I'm insensitive with rage.

"The grummets are fighting! Separate them. Pour water over them! Where's the bosun? Where's the *alguacil*?"

Meanwhile we're rolling around on the deck, and Concho is apparently standing over us, jumping around, trying to land kicks on me wherever he can. Finally they're able to get hold of us and tear us apart, and while Alonso—his nose is bleeding—utters wild threats against me and the peon bellows something, I begin to bawl. I bawl snot and water.

Finally Diego de Arana is on the scene. When he sees me in the restraining arms of two peons—my shirtsleeve is half torn off and I'm quite filthy besides—a certain gleam of satisfaction comes into his eyes.

"A fight involving ships' boys and peons! And shortly before landing! It's a little too casual on this ship, it seems to me. This gives us an opportunity to make an example here. Bosun, all men on deck! There will be a *castigo*, a whipping before the mast.—No, I want to hear nothing at all. It's all the same to me who began it. No differences, same justice for all, isn't that right, my good seamen?

"We'll begin with the peon. Concho González, isn't it? And then we'll go up. Alonso Esposito, second. Pedro Fernández we'll leave till last. He is, as we know, somebody special. We'll spoil the landing for you three!"

The crew gathers. It has grown very still. Except for Concho, who bellows like a steer as they tie him to the mast and resists, swearing he's blameless. They tear off his shirt.

I'm just about to faint.

Before the beating begins, they say a Paternoster. They all kneel with bowed heads and murmur the Latin words they don't understand, and even Concho, bound, says nothing more at all but just weeps softly. He knows what's going to happen to him.

At this moment the admiral appears on the aftercastle.

I don't know whether I'm the first to see him. Since we've come about, he has the evening sun at his back and his long shadow falls over the deck below. I look up at him, at the large, sharply outlined silhouette before the brightness, and despite all my misery and fear I see that he's wearing his beret and one of his magnificent cloaks, perhaps the velvet one, and he's looking down on us, and I have only one thought: What a shame that I cannot see those eyes once more before they do it to me.

Gradually they all notice that he's standing there. Their prayer becomes softer, more uncertain, and they look to him and start to stammer, but up there he's folded his hands around his rosary and prays along until the amen. Then he crosses himself, like all of them—and all at once he's down from his high position like a streak of lightning, has planted himself in front of Arana, and is asking sharply, "What's going on here, *señor alguacil*?"

A surge of voices rushes up to him, but he commands silence with a lordly motion of his hand. "I have asked the provost and no one else. Who has permitted you to get off your knees? Down! Speak, Don Diego!"

Arana reports.

I can see Columbus's face in profile. It is very calm under the decorated edge of his cap. But the rosary is gliding through his fingers at a quite unholy tempo.

Then he nods. "I approve your action. There must be discipline on the ship. Unfortunately, you have forgotten something. When the commanding officer is on board, punishments may be undertaken only with his approval. Also, he must be present at the flogging. You are only the executor, *señor*. I am the commanding officer."

Silence.

Arana looks at the deck and chews on his lip. He has made a mistake and overstepped his authority. "I ask your pardon, *almirante*," he begins, but Columbus interrupts him. "I am moving this *castigo* to the next watch, so that the men have a chance to think over their offenses and repent. That should make their punishment more meaningful. The grummet Pedro, as my page, is under my jurisdiction alone. I will punish him separately."

He looks around and meets only downcast eyes.

"Let him go," he says angrily in an undertone to the two who are holding me. Then he grabs me by the shirt, whereby the sleeve tears out even more, and drags me behind him to the *toldilla,* the way someone drags along a recalcitrant dog. The door closes behind us, and from outside Alonso and Concho can now be heard screaming again and cursing and Arana bellowing orders, which the mate repeats.

The admiral takes me by both shoulders and shakes me. "*Stolto!* Damn it all! There's nothing you leave out, eh? You do nothing but make difficulties! A fight! Imbecile! If the *alguacil* is gracious, it's with the end of a rope, otherwise they use the cat!"

I say nothing at all. I stand there and tremble and cry until my nose is running. He putters around, turns his back to me, and says at some point, "When a person can talk with you again, you'll tell me, yes?"

I nod, and then I tear off my sleeve the rest of the way and blow my nose with it and wipe my face. He looks at me disdainfully.

"Don't you have anything else to put on?"

"Yes," I say. "What I had on when I was pushed overboard. They're still hanging on the capstan to dry."

"Very imprudent for someone like you," he remarks angrily, and I don't know what he means. "It's entirely

out of the question for you to go out there right now—
the way you look! I'll keep you in the *toldilla*. Open my
sea chest and get out one of my shirts. Do it now."

I open the chest and look in. Everything is swimming
before my eyes. I don't see any shirts, only the red velvet
cloak and a silk doublet. He'll certainly wear that tomorrow for the visit to the governor's palace.

"Farther down!" he says impatiently. Obediently I dig
with trembling fingers among the materials. Silk, brocade, velvet. Then something rectangular and smooth. I
take it in my hand. It is a many-times folded piece
of parchment. Next to it lie still other writings. Hand-
written books.

"Why are you staring so?" he asks. "It's the secret sea
chart. Only an idiot hides things where anyone will look
for them."

While I combat a feeling of dizziness, he continues.
"Put that back and finally put something on. For the
crew you'd be a found meal like that. But as far as I'm
concerned, it doesn't charm me in the least."

I look down at myself, and for the first time I see that
when my sleeve tore out, the side seam also ripped, and
my entire upper body is open to his view.

He has turned away.

Chapter Eighteen

It can't be avoided. I'm lying on his bed once again.
He picked me up and laid me down there as I was
about to fall over. I'm still wearing my torn shirt. The
other must be lying in the room somewhere. The room
that spins about me when I open my eyes.

When I was hanging in his arms and he was maneu-
vering me between the curtains of his bed, I murmured,
"Your Grace knew?" and he, almost cheerfully, "Do you
think skirts are the only way by which a man recognizes
a woman?"

And now I'm Pedro again. I'm very unhappily Pedro,
the treacherous grummet, who wanted to save his skin
by betraying the secrets of his master.

Meanwhile the others are getting a hiding. I've stuck
my fingers in my ears, but I still hear their screams. I'd

hear them through a hundred layers of unspun wool around my head. The screams and the slap of the rope on the body.

How they must hate me! Pedro received mercy before judgment. A bed instead of a whipping.

The admiral is there, in his velvet cloak and with the golden chains around his neck, observing the *castigo* as the highest judge on his ship, and he will not blink. I am lying here and my teeth are chattering. I am afraid of the moment when he comes back.

Outside it has grown quiet. Then they are saying their Salve Regina, even more discordant than usual. The mood for other songs has probably left them. No one is singing *"Yo me soy la morenica"* anymore. I hear footsteps outside the door, but he doesn't walk like that. I lie as still as I lay when Señores Gutiérrez and de Arana came in to look around. I clench my teeth hard, to stop this mindless chattering and clattering, and firmly close my eyes. Then I hear the deep, gentle voice of Maestro Bernal. "Our lord admiral was of the opinion that I should concern myself about you, Pedro."

The doctor opens the curtains of the bed and looks at me searchingly.

"There are others on board who probably need your help more than I, *maestro*," I say, and am first of all enormously relieved that it is he and no one else.

"They're taken care of, insofar as the law allows for one of the rabble to be taken care of," he replies.

"I'm the most miserable person on this ship," I say, and he says, "Oh, Pedro, I think that isn't the case at all." He opens his leather case, takes out linen and a jar of salve.

I sit up, pressing my palms hard against the bed. "No. No, most certainly not," I say hastily. "There's nothing wrong with me. I'm healthy, *maestro*. More the fright than anything else. A few scratches that'll heal by themselves."

But he doesn't let himself be put off. "I've been ordered," he says quietly. "Don't be afraid. I know."

I let myself fall back. "Where is he?" I ask with eyes closed.

"A sloop has come alongside with news for the admiral," I hear him say. "He's going to San Sebastián today."

"Ah," I say. "Ah, so." He talks on. "They say that the *gobernadora* just left on an inspection tour of the other islands and won't be back for a week. The admiral wants to pray in the Iglesia de la Asunción." And he adds, "It is thus thoroughly unnecessary for you to cry 'ah' and 'ah, so.' You'd make my work easier if you would sit up again and take off your shirt."

I follow his directions silently, and he dabs carefully around me, putting a compress here, stroking on some salve there. I have gooseflesh all over my body and my teeth are beginning to chatter again. "Now, now," he says soothingly. "It's not so bad. Though it's hard to believe, you handed out more in this fight than you took."

Oh, yes, I think. Above all I've brought two men under the rope before the mast. Very heroic. "I'm going to García and with his help will mix a drink for you. That will help you to get over your fear and panic. That's the only victory that you need carry off today. Otherwise there are no more battles. Do you understand?"

I nod. His kindness does me good and torments me at the same time. "Get dressed," he continues. He regards the shreds of my shirt. "But no, that won't do. You should, I think . . . yes, here. I'll help you put it on." Columbus's shirt is made of the finest Burgundian linen, pleated and trimmed with lace, and it immediately slides off my shoulders, since it is made in the Italian manner, with a wide-cut neck. I must make a knot in the side. It lies so cool and soft on my skin, like the clothes I wore when I still lived in Córdoba, in another life.

"I'll leave you alone briefly now," says Bernal, "and I'll come back with the drink. Do not fear. No one will look for you here. The strictest orders have been given. I'll be back with you again right away."

He goes out, and almost at the same time I hear the commands, the piping of the mate, the familiar to-and-fro of life on board. The admiral is leaving the ship. It must surely still be light outside, but here, in this little room with the three tiny windows and behind the curtains of this bed, it's already dusk. The night will come abruptly. They will light the torches, and the sloop will glide into the harbor like a bejeweled treasure.

The doctor comes back, in his hands a pitcher with a steaming mixture. "You must drink it in small swallows," he prescribes. "Then lie back, stretch out, and try to breathe as if the air were the breath of the Lord, which you suck in and must give back. You will soon sleep. You have nothing to fear, but if you like, I'll stay here with you tonight."

"That won't be necessary, *maestro*," I say, and I take a sip of the aromatic drink. "What is this?"

"Only herbs," he answers. "Nothing you need be disgusted by or that violates your rules of living." He expresses it very wisely and carefully.

"You understand drinks and salves," I say. "I wish I could learn these arts from you."

He smiles. "It's true that they are not known to many. They are not taught even in the faculties of medicine of Castile or Paris. I studied in Moorish Granada." He hesitates a moment, then continues, "One must consider very carefully the persons with whom one uses these medications. One is all too quickly suspected of sorcery, you know."

He takes the empty pitcher away from me, then asks if I would like a light, and when I decline, he closes the bed curtains.

"Follow my advice," he says. "Put your hands down beside you as if this bed were a piece of cooling earth. Lie with your whole body, feel how the ship rocks you. Breathe. Breath is a gift of the Lord, who made Heaven and earth. The Lord bless you and keep you, *mi hija*. You will sleep."

MI HIJA. My daughter, he called me, and I have carried it over into my sleep as if it were a bead on a chain of other beads. But in the labyrinth of my dreams it has grown heavier and heavier like the miraculous stone in fairy tales, which grows unexpectedly and suddenly rests like a rock on your shoulder.

Mi hija! My daughter. And then it happens. The boulders make the uncertain feet of my memory trip, and there is the abyss, into which they fall. It is all there again, all of it.

"*Cobre ánimo, mi hija!*" Be brave, my daughter. Those were his last words to me. I was standing on the balcony of our house. He said it in Castilian, not in our language, so that they would understand it. It meant that he himself was brave.

It must now be the same hour as it was then, when they came for him. Just at dawn. They always come for people just at the time when they are most deeply asleep. In the very earliest hours of the morning.

We knew it would happen, sooner or later. We didn't know that the sooner would be so soon.

It was the usual. Someone had denounced him on the rack. They loved him very much in the *judería,* for he was wise and benevolent, and no one wished him ill. But under torture a person will say anything, and when he knows nothing more, some name comes to his lips and he utters it.

So now they said he had spit on the Host and at one celebration of the Sabbath had fastened a Christian child to a cross. My father! Someone had obviously invented that about the Christian child because Rabbi Judah had taken in a little Christian waif and saved her from death. When the child was bigger and he could be sure that she'd live, he'd given her to the authorities so that she could be raised in the Catholic faith.

There was no saving him. Being accused is as good as being dead.

I knew that my father expected me to go away immediately if they arrested him. I was supposed to save myself and a portion of our possessions and go first to our relatives in Segovia and then abroad. But I disobeyed him. I stayed there.

Day after day I went to the Casa Santa, where the torture chambers of the Inquisition were.

There the relatives of the prisoners gathered. When a heretic had recanted or someone had renounced his faith, sometimes the relatives were permitted to provide him with food and drink until the hour of his death, so that the Santa Hermandad would be spared the expense. The daughter of Rabbi Judah was not permitted. My father renounced nothing.

They endeavored to crown the great holidays, whether religious or secular, with an auto-da-fé, the burning of a heretic. In Córdoba in this year of 1492 it was January 6, the high feast of the appearance of the Lord as bringer of light to the heathen and of the love of God into the darkness of the world, that was chosen for offering the people this spectacle.

I'd done nothing, nothing at all, that my father had told me to. I'd been a very disobedient daughter. I ought to have been gone long since, and I should have given the keys to our house to honest Conversos from the inner city so that they could save what there was to be saved. Instead I kept on running to the Casa Santa, over and over again.

I knew that it was the custom after an auto-da-fé to storm the houses of the executed and plunder what had not already been seized and carried away by the Church. Usually there was nothing left. A few surrounding houses would also fall victim to the anger of the crowd, and the relatives of the heretic had better make themselves scarce then, too.

On January 5, the stakes were erected in the plaza in front of one of the churches, and the people joyfully brought twigs to it. It's said that whoever has brought a twig for the burning of a Jew or a heretic earns five years' remission of his sins.

I sat in the half-empty house from which the Brotherhood, the Santa Hermandad, in the name of the tribunal, had already removed everything of value. This house would burn, just as the stake would burn before it. *Cobre ánimo, mi hija.*

On the morning of the sixth, even before the bells rang for early Mass, I put on the clothes of our former stableboy, who'd run away long ago, as soon as it became suspect to work for an unbeliever. Then I went to the plaza. I wanted to see my father just once more.

I stationed myself on the street through which the condemned would be led to their deaths. There were many. All wore the white penitents' shirt with the sign of the flames painted on it and the tall caps. Rabbi Judah came last of all. He was guided by two fellow condemned, because he couldn't see to walk anymore. He hadn't recanted. He hadn't renounced. They had put out his eyes.

I wanted to leave then, but I couldn't. The maelstrom of the crowd sucked me along with it to the plaza and wouldn't let me escape; it tumbled me right up to the front, where already the heat of the fire could be felt. A good wind was blowing. They couldn't suffocate in the smoke first. They burned until the end. I saw them burn. I heard their screams.

How I got back to our house again I don't know. They must have been right on my heels. In our street I was already hearing doors being broken down, crockery breaking, children crying, and adults shouting.

In a cloth I gathered up the Rabbi Judah's silk prayer

shawl and his tefillin, the phylacteries with which pious Jews bind their head and arm for prayer and fortify themselves with the word of the Scriptures. Then I went into the kitchen, where there was still fire smoldering on the hearth. I took a pine splint, lit it, and went into our library. They had left the books, so long as they weren't decorated with silver or gold or didn't have valuable illustrations. Before the mob got there, I'd done my work. The library burned. Books burn even better than men.

I escaped through the back door.

I lost the prayer shawl along the way. When it was evening, I came to a small vineyard that seemed suitable to me. With my bare hands I dug a little hole in the earth and laid my father's tefillin in it. I wanted to bury this day with it. The memory of it. I wanted to survive. I buried the tefillin and prayed at the spot, said kaddish for my father.

Then I stood up and went on. It had helped. Until this very hour. For how can one live with the memory of such a day?

right morning light is pouring through the window of the *toldilla*. It's the changing of the watch on the *Santa María*. I'm on my knees in the admiral's bed, my head pressed against my fists, rocking back and forth. All at once my pain has spread from my heart throughout my entire body. I have a pain in my belly. I have to curl up. I want the words with which my Marta talked away my childhood pains. But surely they only help when you believe in them.

And suddenly I feel something trickling down my legs. I'm bleeding again. The moment I see it, the pains are gone. It's nothing. Nothing special. God forbid, no omen, nothing important. My body is only showing me that it's there and ready to live. And there's nothing to do now but get out of this bed so that it doesn't look like the aftermath of the chicken butchering and help myself from the trunk of Christopher Columbus—that doesn't matter now, either—to some more linens besides the shirt I'm already wearing.

At about the time of the midday watch, I gather we must be running into the port of San Sebastián. I hear the commands. Once in a while García sticks his head in the door and asks if I want anything to eat, but I don't. I don't leave the room.

Soon afterward I hear the admiral come on board again. Obviously he's prayed. I await him here. I now know what I must do.

An officers' conference is taking place outside. The gentlemen from the *Niña* have also been invited to it. Columbus has learned from a coastal vessel in San Sebastián that the *Pinta* hasn't arrived in the shipyards of Gran Canaria, and he's disturbed. Despite the damage, the caravel should have run into Las Palmas yesterday at the latest, having a much shorter distance to cover than the two other ships.

"I'm going to look for the right man," I hear him say. "It doesn't please me that Captain Pinzón is staying out so long. It doesn't please me at all. No, Don Yáñez, I have no desire to hear a defense of your brother from you. There's supposed to be another ship anchored in Gran Canaria, a *nao*, that's said to be very sturdy and has already sailed to Cape Verde. I'll probably lease that."

And then finally he comes in. His glance passes over me, indifferently, it seems to me, but he must still give me some attention, after everything. I am most certainly not so important as the *Pinta*. But at the moment he dragged me into the *toldilla* by my ripped shirtsleeve, away from certain destruction, he began something. It must now be brought to a conclusion.

I do what I decided to. I fall on my knees before him, bow my head, and say, "*Señor el almirante,* I beg a favor of you."

"A favor?" He laughs without looking at me. "I think I've already shown you enough of that."

"A last favor," I correct myself. "Let me leave the ship in the islands."

He's silent as he draws off his gloves and then paces back and forth in the little room.

Then he says softly, "I haven't had much time to think about it until now, but probably that's right, Pedro. You've earned yourself the hatred of an entire ship's crew for escaping a punishment others suffered. I've lived on ships long enough. One day or night they'll get you. And I can't lodge you in the *toldilla* every evening or be your bodyguard for the rest of the voyage. I wouldn't want anyone on the *Santa María* to do anything to you—and not at all what would happen to you if they discover who you are."

I feel the tears leap into my eyes and press my lips

together. Don't cry. This isn't the time for it. I stand and pull back the bed hangings. "It's also because of this," I say.

That doesn't impress him particularly.

He looks at me. "Does this ... this process last very long with you, and is it very heavy?"

I swallow and avoid his eyes.

"Or do you intend to say that this is the first time—" He breaks off. What shall I say to him? Suddenly he blushes, and I feel that the color is also rising in my cheeks.

He turns away.

"There's a fast boat at my disposal in the region of the islands," he says. "I'm going to ship out for Gran Canaria today, and you will accompany me. I have things to dictate and to draw. I need you for that. Orders have already been given to load my chests."

"How shall I thank Your Grace?" I ask softly, and he replies quickly, "Well, that remains to be decided." He looks past me.

"I still have a confession to make."

He makes an impatient, shooing motion. "Yes, yes, and a thousand questions to ask. Very well. I have other things in my head besides your questions and confessions, Pedro, can you grasp that?"

I nod dumbly. I know that only too well.

"Are you ready? I'm being rowed over to the boat." I draw in a breath to answer, and he interrupts me. "No, you will collect nothing, and you will not say any good-byes here. And you will leave this room only at my side, is that clear?"

And again I can only nod.

"Help me," he says in his ordinary tone. "Why are you standing around? Give me the other cloak and the chain. Pack up the writing things, here in the seabag. And stop acting as though someone has done something to you. No one has done anything to you at all. That's the deciding factor, Pedro. And so it should remain, too."

"Yes, sir."

He takes a deep breath. "I hope I can get free of that hyena Gutiérrez on the island. And a few others, too. Are you done? Then come."

And so I leave the *Santa María* without any farewells and proceed to the rope ladder under the eyes of the crew, who tonight will finally gain their well-earned shore leave. I'm laden with the seabag and stumble behind my stately admiral, a loaded-down figure in a knotted shirt of Burgundian linen, whose sleeves I must roll up three times to allow my fingertips to show.

A laughable figure, an oaf following a grandee.

CHANGING WINDS, calm, slight breeze—thus we amble along. A travel tempo that in no way corresponds to the admiral's expectations. On this tour eastward to the harbor of Las Palmas my presence is acknowledged with hardly a word, and I gain a deep feeling of my own superfluousness. No thoughts of secretarial work, not to mention talking with each other. But at least I don't have to be in constant fear for my life.

There's no cabin here, only an airy tent on the poop in which the admiral stays with his sea chests and instruments when he isn't trying to explain to the captain how one sails.

I have my place in front of it on a mat that the attentive, courteous crew has placed at the disposal of the seafarer's page, and I sleep better than I ever have in the ten days of our crossing—except, of course, when I was lying behind the white curtains.

What he intends for me, when he will open the cage and let the bird fly and under what circumstances, is known only to the Lord God. As for me, I intend to admit my treachery before we part. It isn't necessary to carry everything away with you. Sins can also be banished into the wasteland. Maybe that lets you live.

I have hardly anything to do. I bring him his meals, which the *despensero* gives me, but he doesn't allow himself to be served and waves me away without looking at me. And he's certainly right in that, for I wouldn't look at myself, either. Even if I had a mirror.

At least there's someone here who's as small as I am and so, thanks to the orders of my master, I'm again wearing the normal trousers and coarse shirt of a sailor, and I've even tied a rope around my waist again. After all, you never know when it might come in handy.

Once we're in the harbor of Las Palmas, he rushes off the ship like a whirlwind and to the shipyard and every corner of the harbor, only to determine that there is no *Pinta*, that there also is no ship for hire, and that the *gobernadora*'s ship, according to information from the harbormaster, just yesterday departed in the direction of Lanzarote. Failure all around, and the mood is as expected. Really, he now only needs to wave a hand and say, "God bless you, Pedro, that's all. May all go well with you." But he doesn't do that, either.

Then—miracle of God!—the severely injured *Pinta* lumbers into port, and although the admiral has been ready to impute to Captain Pinzón every kind of insubordination, malice, and sabotage and has almost assumed that Don Martín sailed on alone to discover the fabled lands of gold, it is still only a matter of the broken rudder and contrary winds. And we have our *Pinta* again.

This evening I'm summoned into the tent to prepare important letters to be sent back to Castile. The one to son Diego is also still simmering somewhere. But now, for the first time, there's official mail, primarily reports to Santángel, which I find incredibly false and highly colored. But that really has nothing to do with me now.

The wind blows through the tent we're in on this yacht, unlike the stuffy cabin on the *Santa María*. The wax lights flutter and threaten to go out, and the admiral orders in horn lanterns, in whose uncertain light I continue writing as well as I can. How remarkable it is that we ourselves are spending the night on a ship, when it would be an easy matter to find quarters there in the city. . . .

When we've finished our work, Columbus leans back, stretches out his legs, and crosses his hands behind his head.

"I'm pleased with you, Pedro," he says. "I'll miss you. Yes, really."

"When does Your Grace intend to send me off the ship?" I ask with bated breath.

He shrugs. "Tomorrow, the day after, the day after that," he replies vaguely. We are quiet. The small waves of the harbor basin splash against the side of the ship. "What's that song?" he asks. " 'Whither goest thou, disconsolate one'?"

"I didn't know Your Grace took any notice at all when I told you that someone pushed me overboard."

"I notice more than most wish I did, Pedro." He has closed his eyes.

This is my moment. "I won't leave without asking Your Grace's pardon for what I intended to do," I say seriously.

"What was so dreadful that you intended?" he asks quietly. "Did you intend to hand over my secret sea chart to the enemy?"

"If Señor Gutiérrez and the *alguacil* are the enemies, *señor*, then indeed I intended that," I answer, calm in the expectation of the storm about to break over me.

For a moment nothing happens at all. Then he says, "But Pedro, why do you tell me that? I knew it anyway."

I feel as if someone has hit me in the stomach. I gasp for air. "How does Your Grace mean that?" I ask with difficulty. "Did you regard me as a traitor from the beginning?"

He stands up and begins his usual pacing back and forth. "This is tiresome," he says. "I was so peaceful. Now you come along with your tales and force me. Very well, so be it. I am, as you well know, Genoese. They throw it at me often enough, as if it were a defect to come from a city where a person knows where his advantage lies. I understand that one must come to terms with the world. When someone is as threatened as you, Pedro, he must try to save himself. Somehow someone on the *Santa María* denounced you, I take it. I don't want to know who. You tried to escape. I expected that. Therefore the documents were no longer in the strongbox."

I'm standing in front of him, fists clenched. "So that was all a game? You let me run onto an open knife with the key that I took when you were in your bath, with—" My voice breaks.

"Pedro, hey, Pedro!" he says soothingly. "This way you were safe. You didn't find anything. I prevented anything that might otherwise have happened. There is no Santa Hermandad in the Canaries, and the woman who has the say here hates the Brotherhood, with good reason. So calm down. You would have voyaged to the Jewish kingdoms with me if you hadn't started this mischief with the mob."

Behind my eyeballs the tears that I will not shed are glowing like sparks.

"Excuse me, Don Cristóbal. But tricks like that are strange to me. I come from a family in which a yes is a yes and a no is a no. I come from people who do not break oaths."

"And I come from people who have broken oaths hundreds of times," he says, and there's sharpness in his tone. "Forsworn, perjured themselves, defrauded, lied. Dreadful, isn't it?

"And I am alive. We've been able to acknowledge our Lord Jesus Christ without forgetting the God of our Fathers. What are oaths in the land of Gog and Magog, the land that brings terror and violence to us and to our fathers? And now I'm going to a different land. Perhaps it really is a different land. And you must leave the ship."

"Yes," I say wearily. "I must leave the ship."

"But certainly not without knowing the story of this chart!" he says, and he sounds disappointed. Here I am torturing my conscience for having betrayed him. And he only wants to entrust one of his many secrets to me. Maybe entrusting no one with his secret is just as bad as a hole in the past, a hole in which a few tefillin lie buried.

Everything in me hurts, but it isn't so very bad. It's as if someone had taken a malignant growth out of me and now the hurt places still have to heal. That takes a little time.

"It was many years ago," he begins, and I'm alarmed, for he has his storyteller's voice, the voice he uses to convince, and so I fear I'm going to hear a Moorish fairy tale. He sits there with me crouching at his feet. I lift my head and look at him. He stops. "Oh," he says, "it's utterly and completely the truth. Not one of those things involving saints or sorcerers."

I gulp. Is he reading minds again?

He continues.

"Many years ago I was married to a woman, a Portuguese, whose family was noble but utterly impoverished. Still, her brother had the hereditary governorship of Porto Santo. That's a small island in the vicinity of Madeira, north of us, about as many leagues removed from this spot as we are from Spain. We settled there, and it was very dull, even though in the absences of my brother-in-law I was the governor there and exercised jurisdiction. But the jurisdiction over a handful of vegetable farmers is quite pathetic compared to the power one has as commander of a ship. I saw to it that I received as many commissions taking me away from there as possible.

"The island had a peculiarity, Pedro. On its west coast there is a strong, constantly warm current, and there are often strange seeds and timbers washed up there, pinecones such as I've never seen before, also carved sticks. These things must have come from the islands on the other side of the sea. Evidence that the islands were there!

"And then, one day—God had already called Doña Felipa to Him, and I was sitting there on this handful of sand and stones saddled with a little three-year-old son and nothing else—there, where I often stood staring to the west, squinting as if some sort of land contour might appear in the distance, a boat washed up, and in it was a handful of dying men.

"They were the last survivors of a Portuguese caravel that had set out for Guinea a long time before. At that time the Portuguese were sailing a secret detour on the high seas to avoid the Spanish privateers. There's an area called 'mother of the storms.' The caravel, I learned, was caught in a tornado and ran before the wind, sails reefed, farther and farther toward the west, faster than a ship has ever sailed before, the bow wave as high as a house on both sides."

Again his voice has taken on that dreamy tone, as if he's describing not a horror but a celestial miracle, and I interrupt him carefully. "How did you learn this?"

"From the navigator of the caravel. I took him in with me. He died in my house. They all died, famished, half dead of thirst, haggard with illness, and consumed by strange fevers. But they had been there. They'd seen it." His voice is now almost a whisper. One of his hands—

he's been using them animatedly as he speaks—lands on my head as if by accident. He touches my short hair carefully and gently.

"The land is fruitful and green. The people are brown-skinned and friendly. They exchange gold for trinkets, for they don't understand the value of it. These are the islands that lie before India. The Portuguese cruised there for months, and it was, he said, like Paradise. But then worms ate the hull of the ship and disease the bodies of the men. With their last strength they set out on the return voyage. West of Madeira the ship broke up, and the sailors saved themselves in the boat.

"He told me all this on his deathbed, and at first I thought that it was the fever talking. But then I found it in his seabag. The chart with the lines of the coast, the route by which one reaches it. The logbook with the notations: anchorages, landmarks, watering places, everything. And the people there told them that the sea went on further to the west. One can sail on."

"And you kept it after his death?"

"Of course," he says calmly. "I kept it and told no one of it. Flotsam belongs to the finder, and this navigator, whose last confession I heard and whose eyes I closed, was my flotsam. Besides, what else was I to do? You know that in Spain and Portugal the collection of navigation data and sea charts is the prerogative of the Crown. A foreigner with such material in his possession—I would have vanished into the dungeons, Pedro."

His long, strong fingers travel over the back of my head and my neck.

"Since then I've known that I'd get there. But not like the voyagers of the North, with a single ship in order to tell tales later in the bars of the harbor cities that might be believed or not. No, if I were to travel there, it would be with the blessing of Heaven and the mandate of the Crown. Gold, power, and honor for me and my descendants would be certain. And: hope for the adherents of the Old Testament."

"But the people there, you say . . ."

"The people of whom the navigator spoke are only the inhabitants of the islands that lie before the real realms of the East. I'm going to sail on and find them."

He is constantly stroking me, lost in thought. But I don't know if he's thinking of me at all. He's frowning.

"You won't be there, Pedro, so I can confide something to you, something that no one may know. Otherwise they'd probably run away from me in droves—not only those on whom I reckon, anyway, for I think some of them only wanted to come with me this far and others have grown afraid in view of the ocean before us. We're penetrating deep into Portuguese territory."

"Into enemy territory?" I ask breathlessly.

He nods. "As you know, His Holiness Pope Alexander established a line of separation between Portuguese and Spanish sovereign waters. Any ship of the respective states that ventures into the territory of the other can be seized or sunk. The captains can be taken prisoner and publicly hanged.

"To avoid currents and winds, it's imperative we first head to the south and then west," he says matter-of-factly. "Therefore we're keeping—I'm keeping—two log-books. If anyone inspects us, we can prove that I never left Castilian waters. We're only sailing west."

"But that can mean death," I murmur.

"Only if they catch you," he replies.

What a game! And who am I in this undertaking? An annoyance.

Our lanterns flare up and go out, first one, then the other. The oil is all burned up.

"Does Your Grace command that I light more—"

His hand presses me down. "Right now I command only that you sit here and keep still." The fingers glide over my shoulder and my arm.

"You know what you're doing, Don Cristóbal?"

He sighs. "Yes, *donzella,* unfortunately I know it all too well. And therefore I must now stop it."

Donzella. Girl. Maiden. As tender and playful as the drawings he made in the margin of the manuscript.

"At your service, *señor el almirante,*" I whisper.

"No," he says. He turns me toward him, and in the dull gleam of the ship's lanterns outside I see his very grave eyes. "Not at my service. I would now either hurt you very much or frighten you very much. Perhaps both. That is not good."

"Ah," I reply, "I've been running around in these clothes for half a year. I know quite a lot about men."

He repeats a saying that I know from the public houses: "One thing to know, another thing to do." At the same time he takes his hand off my shoulder, but I reach for it. He sighs again, bites his lip, shakes his head, and withdraws his hand.

"It's because of that other woman, isn't it?" I ask, my voice choked.

"Your question proves to me, *donzella,* that you really know nothing at all about men." He stands up. "Go sleep, Pedro. Outside there in front of the tent. This isn't our hour. It shall not be this way."

Who decides to whom an hour belongs? I wanted this one.

Chapter Twenty

The next day he's busy at the shipyard, overseeing the repairs to the *Pinta,* and evidently he and Captain Pinzón have more difficulties with each other. He declares to me in the evening with cold fury that he'd like to fasten Pinzón to the doorposts of his house with his own hands when they get back to Palos again—as if they're only intending to sail to Cadiz and back, or something. I don't understand at all what it was about and also don't listen very carefully.

In the morning I'm sent out to the market to buy for myself what I need here. Of course the admiral has no money in his purse and borrows it—or demands it—from the captain of our yacht.

I have to learn to walk on land all over again. First of all I acquire espadrilles of goatskin for my feet, for there are many stones here; a woolen cape and a kerchief; a wallet that I can hang around my neck, even if I have nothing to put in it; a comb, a knife, a spoon.

In the market there are strange folk in skins, who obviously don't know any Spanish and avert their eyes if you try to speak to them.

The island is green and rugged, and where the rocks protrude it is brown or black. There is a church in Las Palmas, two bars, and a whorehouse. All around is the sea. I see plants that I've never seen before in my life.

The wind blows softly, and it is not hot.

It is a strange country, where I know no one and no one wants anything of me, good or bad.

In the evening my admiral is angry. Again nothing is going fast enough, and Pinzón is, I am told, such a scoundrel that I wonder how Columbus ever intends to sail even one league more with him.

"When I've found the lands, he has to leave!" When he says that, it sounds as if he just put the lands down somewhere in his sea chest. Yesterday's talk seems forgotten.

"As I see it, Pedro, you've already provided yourself with what you need," he remarks. With what I need! A pair of shoes, a knife, a cape, a wallet . . . merciful God.

"You still need something else from me," he says. "You're a person who attracts difficulties. You should have a letter of protection from me for all eventualities. I'll dictate it to you.

"So, write: To the *gobernadora* of the Canary Islands,

Doña Beatriz de Bobadilla, from her loyal servant, Cristóbal Colón, admiral of the ocean seas.

"Señora of my heart and all my senses, I kiss your beneficent hands."

He stops. "What's the matter? Can't you follow?"

"I won't write that," I say, crossing my arms over my chest.

"You will write what's dictated to you!" he bellows. Then he stops, looks fixedly at me, and bursts into laughter. It's the first time I've heard him laugh aloud. But he's not laughing with me but at me. "Pedro!" he says, the way you talk to a child. "Pick up the quill and write, all right? This is being done for you, you understand?" He lifts his finger and taps me on the forehead three times. "Tock-tock-tock. For you, Pedrito! *Capisce?*"

I'm almost in tears. I press my lips together and pick up the pen again, and he continues: "So, if you have that, then: The carrier of this letter, Doña—insert your name there—is for various reasons very dear to me. So, under whatever circumstances she may reach you and whatever is said about her, I beg Your Grace in your high capacity as governor of the islands for protection and assistance for the above-named person. I commend myself to your favor, most beautiful of all women. Your cavalier—and now give it to me so that I can sign it." He dips the quill and writes his signature in his clear, sweepingly ornamented manner, as if he were signing a document of great importance.

"Sprinkle it with sand," he commands. "Sealing wax. Fold the letter. So. You will always carry this with you, as long as you are in these islands. I order you to. Wrap it in a waxed linen cloth and carry it in your wallet. Understand?"

He grasps my chin and forces me to look him in the eyes. It is the last time I'll see the ocean in those gray eyes. "Is Your Grace worried about me?" I ask.

"I don't know," he replies. "You get into difficulties, you get out. Take it that I expect to see you again." He lets me go. His touch was rough, and his eyes are imperious.

"I thank Your Grace," I say tonelessly.

"Don't play the martyr," he snaps at me. "You're alive, aren't you? It's comfortable here. Consider whether you want to stay here on Gran Canaria or come back to Gomera with me. But I wouldn't advise you to go to Gomera. You should avoid ever being seen again by the crew of the *Santa María*. But it's your decision. Decide by tomorrow. I intend to go back. Also, the climate is very pleasant here."

"I didn't leave Spain because of the climate," I say angrily. "Your Grace really should know that." He turns around, and I fear that I'm already getting into more trouble this very evening.

But I stand firm. "Permit me one more question."

"Ah, your questions. Yes, of course. Ask your question."

"Did you really leave the key for me when you took the bath?"

"For Heaven's sake!" he says, fanning the air with his hand. "I want to tell you one thing, Pedro: You take yourself too seriously. That's it. Whether I did it for you or it was only an accident—what difference does it make? Things aren't the way you'd like them to be."

"How, in Your Grace's opinion, would I like things to be?"

"You would like them to be simple. But they are complex and fractured."

"Things aren't!" I say, becoming more and more excited. "It's people who make what you call things. But the Lord God doesn't intend for there to be so many lies in the world!"

"Next you'll be explaining to me what the Lord God and Our Savior Jesus Christ have in mind for humankind!"

"About the latter I know nothing," I say, swallowing tears, and think that now I'll certainly get my ears boxed again. But then in the west, where the sun has just gone down, a pillar of fire goes up and a deep growl like that of ten thunderstorms suddenly rushes across the arc of the sky. I shriek in terror, and Columbus crosses himself and looks in fascination at the place where the uncanny sight appeared.

"I hope no one gets the idea to consider that an omen

for the undertaking!" he murmurs. "Otherwise more men will jump ship than I can replace here...."

He springs up and begins negotiating feverishly with the captain. I stare at the cascades of flames.

"Come, Pedro," he says. "I've given orders to lower the boat. First of all I must talk with the people on the *Pinta*. Then I have to go straight to Gomera. I have to explain to them all that it's nothing out of the ordinary."

"Could you also explain it to me? I'm terribly frightened."

We're already down the rope ladder and into the boat.

"It's subterranean fire," he says. "A volcano. The Lord opens it whenever He wants to. It has nothing to do with omens or portents. They exist everywhere. There's Bartolomé de Torres on the *Santa María*. He's sailed with me to Iceland, where they also exist. He knows it and will reassure the men. And there's a Venetian serving on the *Niña*. He must know of Stromboli, on the west coast of Italy, which shoots its fire into the sky at all hours. We're all God's creatures, and to Him we return."

He is calm, collected, decided. Arrow-straight, like a ship when it's running before the wind.

The pillar of fire stands there before us while we're being rowed to the quay, like the one that led Moses and the people through the desert. He uses the signs as he needs them. He doesn't want this one. I don't either.

He hurries with long steps to the shipyard and to the streets in the harbor where his sailors are gathered and looking toward him. Certainly the fiery tongues of his cajoling will flicker over them like the flames over this mountain so that he'll calm them and keep them from running away.

I have everything with me. Cape and kerchief. A wallet with a comb and knife and a remarkable letter of protection, which I only picked up because it's signed by his hand.

Now he doesn't even notice that I'm gone. Now he doesn't miss me. Later perhaps, I hope.

Now I'm finally free. One can't get any freer. Free of all possessions, naked and bare like a newly hatched fly on the wall of a wooden shed. Free of all ties. Free of that man who consoled me and humiliated me, raised me and trod me into the dust, and finally saved me. Not free of my feelings for him.

Not free of love, not free of hate. But the grief weighs the heaviest. I sit here between a column of fire behind me and an ocean in front of me, on bare rock, on an island on which I know no human being. I have lost not only him, but all my people. Of all those who renounced their faith in order to be able to leave Spain, who gave up all their possessions in order to flee, the poorest are those who are alone, without their relatives and friends. All at once it occurs to me that now, except when I pray to God, I will never again speak Hebrew, the language that has bound Jews together all over the world and has united them, the most valuable of all valuables, the only thing they could take out of Castile unmolested. What is it our wise men say? "O, thou holy language, I adore thee. Even should my people be taken captive, I can well comfort myself with thee, Beloved."

And suddenly the tears flood down my face like an overflowing spring. *"Shema yisrael,"* I pray, *"adonai elohenu, adonai echod,"* saying the chief prayer of my father and forefathers, calling on the name of God, of the Lord, and blessing him who sails over the sea in order to find hope for us—maybe.

Farewell, Cristóbal Colón. May the God of Israel guide you. Didn't you say you thought you'd see me again?

Well, I want that, too. So I'm not entirely disconsolate.

THE YEAR 1492 is fixed in our memories as the year of the discovery of America by Christopher Columbus.

However, at least in the history of Spain, this year is associated with two other historical events—violent and bloody events. In this year Their Catholic Majesties Ferdinand and Isabella defeated the Islamic kingdom of Granada in southern Spain and drove the Moors out of the country. Only the Jews now stood in the way of the creation of a "purely" Christian nation. That same year, by decree, the Jews, too, were expelled from the country, every single one, if they did not convert to Christianity. And here, in their methods, the Spanish Inquisitors proved themselves worthy antecedents of the fascist persecutors of the twentieth century.

But now, what connection do these events have with

Columbus's voyage of discovery? These questions were investigated by the famous historian and journalist Simon Wiesenthal—the man who hunted down the Nazi criminal Adolf Eichmann—in a book that is just as astute as it is spectacular. The book is called *Sails of Hope*. Wiesenthal bundled together, so to speak, the host of riddles and speculations about Columbus's origins, his motivations, and the background of his support at the court of Their Spanish Majesties. Wiesenthal's conclusions—namely, that Columbus probably had Jewish forebears and that his protectors and patrons were baptized Jews who had well-founded interests in discovering the prophesied "Jewish kingdoms" beyond the seas—are of compelling logic, a logic that has convinced not only me but other historians since then.

Further novelties in my book are the discoveries about the meaning of Columbus's falsification of the log, the true reasons that made him take the course that he chose, and possible predecessors on the journey to the Indies—or to new lands. Here I was inspired by John Dyson (writer), Peter Christopher (photographer), and Luís Miguel Coín Cuenca (sailor), who with a crew of young Spanish sea officers sailed a replica of the *Niña* along Columbus's route and developed their theses.

The questions about the explorer will never end, and certainly many more theories will evolve and many more portraits of Columbus will be sketched. This one is mine.

—WALDTRAUT LEWIN

BEFORE SHE TURNED TO WRITING, Waldtraut Lewin studied Germanic languages, theater, and Latin in Berlin and then had a career as a music dramaturge, opera director, and translator of operas by Handel. She has always been particularly interested in historical material. Her first historical novel appeared in 1972, followed by many others. Several were honored with prizes, including the Lion-Feuchtwanger-Preis, the national prize of the former German Democratic Republic.

ELIZABETH D. CRAWFORD's translations have won many awards, including the Mildred L. Batchelder Award in 1998 for *The Robber and Me* by Josef Holub. She lives in Orange, Connecticut.